OLD FRENCH FAIRY TALES

ROSALIE SAW BEFORE HER EYES A TREE OF MARVELOUS BEAUTY

—*Page 171*

OLD FRENCH FAIRY TALES

BY

COMTESSE DE SEGUR

ILLUSTRATED BY

VIRGINIA FRANCES STERRETT

Fredonia Books
Amsterdam, The Netherlands

Old French Fairy Tales

by
Comtesse de Segur

ISBN: 1-4101-0569-5

Reprinted from the 1920 edition

Fredonia Books
Amsterdam, The Netherlands
http://www.fredoniabooks.com

In order to make original editions of historical works available to scholars at an economical price, this facsimile of the original edition of 1920 is reproduced from the best available copy and has been digitally enhanced to improve legibility, but the text remains unaltered to retain historical authenticity.

THE STORIES

BLONDINE. BONNE-BICHE, AND BEAU-MINON

GOOD LITTLE HENRY

PRINCESS ROSETTE

THE LITTLE GRAY MOUSE

OURSON

ILLUSTRATIONS

Blondine Bonne Biche and Beau Minon

THE STORY OF BLONDINE, BONNE-BICHE, AND BEAU-MINON

BLONDINE

THERE was once a king called Benin. He was good and all the world loved him; he was just and the wicked feared him. His wife, the Queen Doucette, was also good, and much beloved.

This happy pair had a daughter called the Princess Blondine, because of her superb fair hair, and she was as amiable and charming as her father the king and her mother the queen.

Unfortunately, the poor queen died a short time after the birth of Blondine and for a long time the king wept bitterly at his great loss. Blondine was too young to understand her mother's death: she did not weep but continued to laugh, to play and to sleep peacefully. The king loved her tenderly and she loved him more than all the world. He gave his little daughter the most beautiful jewels, the finest bonbons, and the most rare and delicious fruits. Blondine was very happy.

One day it was announced to the king, that all his subjects demanded that he should marry again in order to have a son who should reign after him. He refused at first but finally yielded to the pressing desires of his people and said to his minister Leger:—

"My dear friend, my subjects wish me to marry again but my heart is so sad because of the death of my cherished queen Doucette that I cannot undertake the task of seeking another wife. Go, then, my good Leger and find me a princess who will make my sweet Blondine happy. Go; I ask for nothing more. When you have found a perfect woman, you will demand her hand in marriage and conduct her to my court."

Leger set off immediately, visited many courts and saw innumerable princesses—ugly, humpbacked and wicked.

At last he arrived at the kingdom of the monarch Turbulent, who had a lovely daughter, bright, winning and apparently good. Leger found her so charming, that he asked her hand in marriage for his king Benin, without sufficiently inquiring into her real character.

Leger meets the wicked princess, Fourbette

Turbulent was enchanted at the prospect of getting rid of his daughter who was jealous, proud and wicked. Also, her presence often interfered with his excursions for pleasure, with the chase and with his various entertainments at the palace.

Without a moment's hesitation, he acceded to the Prime Minister's request, and he returned with the princess to the kingdom of the good king Benin.

The princess Fourbette was accompanied by four thousand mules, loaded with the jewels and wardrobe of the charming bride.

King Benin had been apprised of their approach by a courier and went forward to receive the princess Fourbette. He found her beautiful but he noted the absence of the mild and attractive expression of the poor lost Doucette.

When Fourbette's eyes fell upon Blondine her glance was so cruel, so wicked, that the poor child, who was now three years old, was greatly terrified and began to weep bitterly.

"What is the matter?" said the king. "Why does my sweet and sensible Blondine weep like a bad little girl?"

"Papa! dear papa!" cried Blondine, throwing herself into the arms of the king, "do not give me into the hands of this princess. I am afraid of her—her eyes are cruel!"

The king was much surprised. He turned so suddenly towards the princess Fourbette that she had no time to control herself and he perceived the terrible glance with which she regarded the little Blondine.

Benin immediately resolved that Blondine should be wholly separated from the new queen and remain as before under the exclusive protection of the nurse who had taken care of her and who loved her tenderly.

The queen thus saw Blondine rarely, and when she met

her by chance she could not wholly dissimulate the hatred she felt for her.

About a year from that time a daughter was born to the queen Fourbette. She was named Brunette, because of her dark hair which was black as the raven's wing.

Brunette was pretty but not so lovely as Blondine; moreover she was as wicked as her mother. She detested Blondine and played all sorts of cruel tricks upon her, bit her, pinched her, pulled her hair, broke her toys and tore her beautiful dresses.

The good little Blondine was never in a passion with her sister but always tried to make excuses for her conduct.

"Oh, papa!" she said to the king, "do not scold Brunette; she is so little! she does not know that she grieves me when she breaks my toys! It is only in play that she bites me, pulls my hair and pinches me."

The good king embraced his little daughter, and was silent but he knew that Brunette was cruel and wicked; that Blondine was too gentle and good to accuse her. He loved Blondine, therefore, more and more from day to day and his heart grew cold to Brunette.

The ambitious queen Fourbette saw all this clearly and hated intensely the innocent and gentle Blondine. If she had not feared the rage of the king she would have made Blondine the most wretched child in the world.

Benin had commanded that Blondine should never be

left alone with the queen. He was known to be just and good but he punished disobedience severely and the queen herself dared not defy his commands.

BLONDINE LOST

BLONDINE grew to be seven years old and Brunette three.

The king had given Blondine a charming little carriage drawn by ostriches, and a little coachman ten years of age, who was the nephew of her nurse.

The little page, who was called Gourmandinet, loved Blondine tenderly. He had been her playmate from her birth and she had shown him a thousand acts of kindness.

But Gourmandinet had one terrible fault; he was a gourmand—was so fond of dainties and sweet things, that for a paper of bonbons he would commit almost any wicked action. Blondine often said to him:

"I love you dearly, Gourmandinet, but I do not love to

see you so greedy. I entreat you to correct this villainous fault which will make you despised by all the world."

Gourmandinet kissed her hand and promised to reform. But, alas! he continued to steal cakes from the kitchen and bonbons from the store-room. Often, indeed, he was whipped for his disobedience and gluttony.

The queen Fourbette heard on every hand the reproaches lavished upon the page and she was cunning enough to think that she might make use of this weakness of Gourmandinet and thus get rid of poor Blondine.

The garden in which Blondine drove in her little carriage, drawn by ostriches and guided by her little coachman, Gourmandinet, was separated by a grating from an immense and magnificent forest, called the Forest of Lilacs because during the whole year these lilacs were always covered with superb flowers.

No one, however, entered these woods. It was well known that it was enchanted ground and that if you once entered there you could never hope to escape.

Gourmandinet knew the terrible secret of this forest. He had been severely forbidden ever to drive the carriage of Blondine in that direction lest by some chance Blondine might pass the grating and place her little feet on the enchanted ground.

Many times the king Benin had sought to build a wall the entire length of the grating or to secure it in some way so as to make an entrance there impossible. But the workmen had no sooner laid the foundation than some unknown and invisible power raised the stones and they disappeared from sight.

The queen Fourbette now sought diligently to gain the friendship of Gourmandinet by giving him every day some delicious dainties. In this way she made him so complete a slave to his appetite that he could not live without the jellies, bonbons and cakes which she gave him in such profusion. At last she sent for him to come to her, and said:—

"Gourmandinet, it depends entirely upon yourself whether you shall have a large trunk full of bonbons and delicious dainties or never again eat one during your life."

"Never again eat one! Oh! madam, I should die of such punishment. Speak, madam, what must I do to escape this terrible fate?"

"It is necessary," said the queen, looking at him fixedly, "that you should drive the princess Blondine near to the Forest of Lilacs."

"I cannot do it, madam; the king has forbidden it."

"Ah! you cannot do it; well, then, adieu. No more dainties for you. I shall command every one in the house to give you nothing."

"Oh! madam," said Gourmandinet, weeping bitterly, "do not be so cruel. Give me some order which it is in my power to execute."

"I can only repeat that I command you to lead the princess Blondine near to the Forest of Lilacs; that you encourage her to descend from the carriage, to cross the grating and enter the enchanted ground."

"But, madam," replied Gourmandinet, turning very pale, "if the princess enters this forest she can never escape from it. You know the penalty of entering upon enchanted ground. To send my dear princess there is to give her up to certain death."

"For the third and last time," said the queen, frowning fearfully, "I ask if you will take the princess to the forest? Choose! either an immense box of bonbons which I will renew every month or never again to taste the delicacies which you love."

"But how shall I escape from the dreadful punishment which his majesty will inflict upon me?"

"Do not be disquieted on that account. As soon as you have induced Blondine to enter the Forest of Lilacs, return to me. I will send you off out of danger with your bonbons, and I charge myself with your future fortune."

"Oh! madam, have pity upon me. Do not compel me to lead my dear princess to destruction. She who has always been so good to me!"

"You still hesitate, miserable coward! Of what importance is the fate of Blondine to you? When you have obeyed my commands I will see that you enter the service of

Brunette and I declare to you solemnly that the bonbons shall never fail."

Gourmandinet hesitated and reflected a few moments longer and, alas! at last resolved to sacrifice his good little mistress to his gluttony.

The remainder of that day he still hesitated and he lay awake all night weeping bitter tears as he endeavored to discover some way to escape from the power of the wicked queen; but the certainty of the queen's bitter revenge if he refused to execute her cruel orders, and the hope of rescuing Blondine at some future day by seeking the aid of some powerful fairy, conquered his irresolution and decided him to obey the queen.

In the morning at ten o'clock Blondine ordered her little carriage and entered it for a drive, after having embraced the king her father and promised him to return in two hours.

The garden was immense. Gourmandinet, on starting, turned the ostriches away from the Forest of Lilacs. When, however, they were entirely out of sight of the palace, he changed his course and turned towards the grating which separated them from the enchanted ground. He was sad and silent. His crime weighed upon his heart and conscience.

"What is the matter?" said Blondine, kindly. "You say nothing. Are you ill, Gourmandinet?"

"No, my princess, I am well."

"But how pale you are! Tell me what distresses you, poor boy, and I promise to do all in my power to make you happy."

Blondine's kind inquiries and attentions almost softened the hard heart of Gourmandinet, but the remembrance of the bonbons promised by the wicked queen, Fourbette, soon chased away his good resolutions. Before he had time to reply, the ostriches reached the grating of the Forest of Lilacs.

"Oh! the beautiful lilacs!" exclaimed Blondine; "how fragrant—how delicious! I must have a bouquet of those beautiful flowers for my good papa. Get down, Gourmandinet and bring me some of those superb branches."

"I cannot leave my seat, princess, the ostriches might run away with you during my absence."

"Do not fear," replied Blondine; "I could guide them myself to the palace."

"But the king would give me a terrible scolding for having abandoned you, princess. It is best that you go yourself and gather your flowers."

"That is true. I should be very sorry to get you a scolding, my poor Gourmandinet."

While saying these words she sprang lightly from the carriage, crossed the bars of the grating and commenced to gather the flowers.

At this moment Gourmandinet shuddered and was overwhelmed with remorse. He wished to repair his fault by calling Blondine but although she was only ten steps from him,—although he saw her perfectly—she could not hear his voice, and in a short time she was lost to view in the enchanted forest.

For a long time Gourmandinet wept over his crime, cursed his gluttony and despised the wicked queen Fourbette.

At last he recalled to himself that the hour approached at which Blondine would be expected at the palace. He returned to the stables through the back entrance and ran at once to the queen, who was anxiously expecting him.

On seeing him so deadly pale and his eyes inflamed from the tears of awful remorse, she knew that Blondine had perished.

"Is it done?" said she.

Gourmandinet bowed his head. He had not the strength to speak.

"Come," said she, "behold your reward!"

She pointed to a large box full of delicious bonbons of every variety. She commanded a valet to raise the box and place it upon one of the mules which had brought her jewelry.

"I confide this box to Gourmandinet, in order that he may take it to my father," she said. "Go, boy, and return in a month for another." She placed in his hand at the same time a purse full of gold.

Gourmandinet mounted the mule in perfect silence and set off in full gallop. The mule was obstinate and wilful and soon grew restive under the weight of the box and began to prance and kick. He did this so effectually that he threw Gourmandinet and his precious box of bonbons upon the ground.

Gourmandinet, who had never ridden upon a horse or mule, fell heavily with his head upon the stones and died instantly.

Thus he did not receive from his crime the profit which he had hoped, for he had not even tasted of the bonbons which the queen had given him.

No one regretted him. No one but the poor Blondine had ever loved him.

THE FOREST OF LILACS

WHEN Blondine entered the forest she commenced gathering the beautiful branches of lilacs. She rejoiced in their profusion and delighted in their fragrance.

As she made her selection, it seemed to her that those which were more distant were still more beautiful so she emptied her apron and her hat, which were both full and filled them again and again.

Blondine had been thus busily occupied for about an hour. She began to suffer from the heat and to feel great fatigue. She found the branches of lilacs heavy to carry and thought it was time to return to the palace. She looked around and saw herself surrounded with lilacs. She called Gourmandinet but no one replied.

"I have wandered further than I intended," said Blondine. "I will return at once, though I am very weary. Gourmandinet will hear me and will surely come to meet me."

Blondine walked on rapidly for some time but she could not find the boundaries of the forest.

Many times she called anxiously upon Gourmandinet but he did not respond and at last she became terribly frightened.

"What will become of me, all alone in this vast forest? What will my poor papa think when I do not return? And Gourmandinet, how will he dare go back to the palace without me? He will be scolded, perhaps beaten and all this is my fault because I would leave my carriage to gather lilacs? Unfortunate girl that I am! I shall die of hunger and thirst in this forest if the wolves do not eat me up this night."

Weeping bitterly, Blondine fell on the ground at the foot of a large tree. She wept a long time. At last her great fatigue mastered her grief. She placed her little head upon her bundle of lilacs, and slept peacefully.

BLONDINE'S AWAKENING—BEAU-MINON

BLONDINE slept calmly all night; no ferocious beast came to trouble her slumbers. She did not suffer from the cold and awakened at a late hour in the morning. She rubbed her eyes, much surprised to see herself surrounded by trees, in place of being in her own room in the palace, and upon her own bed.

She called her nurse and a soft mewing was the only response. Astonished and almost frightened, she looked around and saw at her feet a superb white cat, looking gently upon her and continuing to mew plaintively.

"Ah! pretty puss! how beautiful you are!" cried Blondine, placing her little hand caressingly upon the soft fur, white as snow. "I am so happy to see you, pretty puss, for you will conduct me to your home. I am indeed very hungry and I have not the strength to walk much further without food."

Blondine had scarcely uttered these words, when the white pussy mewed again and pointed with her little paw to a small package lying near her, wrapped neatly in fine white linen. She opened the parcel and found it contained bread and butter which she found delicious. She gave the crumbs to pussy, who munched them with seeming delight.

When they had finished their simple meal, Blondine leaned over towards her little companion, and said, caressingly:

"Thanks, pretty puss, for the breakfast you have given me. Now, can you conduct me to my papa, who is certainly in despair because of my absence?"

Pussy, whom Blondine named Beau-Minon, shook her head and mewed plaintively.

"Ah! you understand me, Beau-Minon," said Blondine. "I entreat you to have pity upon me and lead me to some house before I perish with hunger, cold and terror in this vast forest!"

Beau-Minon looked at the princess fixedly and made a sign with her little graceful white head which seemed to say, "I understand you." She rose, advanced a few steps and paused to see if Blondine followed her.

"I am here, Beau-Minon; I am following you gladly,"

said Blondine; "but how can we pass through these bushy thickets? I see no path."

Beau-Minon made no reply but sprang lightly into the thicket which opened of itself to allow Blondine and Beau-Minon to pass, and then closed up immediately.

Blondine walked on for about half an hour. As she advanced, the forest became lighter, the grass was finer and the flowers more abundant. She saw many pretty birds singing melodiously and graceful squirrels, bounding along the branches of the trees.

Blondine, who had no doubt that she was about to leave the forest and see her dear father again, was enchanted with all that she saw; she wished to pause and gather the lovely wild flowers; but Beau-Minon advanced steadily and mewed plaintively whenever Blondine relaxed her speed.

In about an hour Blondine perceived an elegant castle. Beau-Minon led her to the gilded grating. However, Blondine did not know how to enter. There was no bell and the gate was closed. Beau-Minon had disappeared and Blondine was once more alone.

BONNE-BICHE

BEAU-MINON had entered by a little passage, which seemed made expressly for him and had probably given notice to some one at the castle, as the gate opened without Blondine having called.

She entered the court-yard but saw no one.

The door of the castle opened of itself. Blondine entered the vestibule which was of rare white marble. All the doors of the castle now opened like the first and the princess passed through a suite of beautiful rooms.

At last, in the back part of a charming salon, furnished with blue and gold, she perceived a white hind, lying upon a bed of fine and fragrant grasses. Beau-Minon stood near her. The pretty hind saw Blondine, arose, and approached her.

"You are most welcome, Blondine," said she. "My son Beau-Minon and I have expected you for a long time."

At these words, Blondine was much frightened.

"Take courage, princess; you are with friends. I know the king your father and I love him and I love you also."

"Oh, madam," said Blondine, "if you know the king my father, I pray you to take me to him. My absence must make him very wretched."

"My dear Blondine," said the hind, whose name was Bonne-Biche, sighing, "it is not in my power to conduct you to your father. You are in the hands of the magician of the Forest of Lilacs. I myself am subject to his power which is superior to mine but I can send soft dreams to your father, which will reassure him as to your fate and let him know that you are safe with me."

"Oh, madam!" said Blondine, in an agony of grief, "shall I never again see my father whom I love so tenderly? My poor father!"

"Dear Blondine, do not distress yourself as to the future. Wisdom and prudence are always recompensed. You will see your father again but not now. In the meantime be good and docile. Beau-Minon and I will do all in our power to make you happy."

Blondine sighed heavily and shed a few tears. She then reflected that to manifest such grief was a poor recompense for all the goodness of Bonne-Biche. She resolved, therefore, to control herself and to be cheerful.

Bonne-Biche took her to see the apartment they had prepared for her. The bedroom was hung with rose-colored silk embroidered with gold. The furniture was covered with white velvet worked with silks of the most brilliant hues. Every species of animal, bird and butterfly were represented in rare embroidery.

Adjoining Blondine's chamber was a small study. It was hung with sky-blue damask, embroidered with fine pearls. The furniture was covered with silver moiré, adorned with nails of turquoise. Two magnificent portraits, representing a young and superbly handsome woman and a strikingly attractive young man, hung on the walls. Their costumes indicated that they were of royal race.

"Whose portraits are these, madam?" said Blondine to Bonne-Biche.

"I am forbidden to answer that question, dear Blondine. You will know later;—but this is the hour for dinner. Come, Blondine, I am sure you are hungry."

Blondine was in fact almost dying of hunger. She followed Bonne-Biche and they entered the dining-room where she saw a table strangely served.

An enormous cushion of black satin was placed on the floor for Bonne-Biche. On the table before her was a vase filled with the choicest herbs, fresh and nutritious and near this vase was a golden bucket, filled with fresh and limpid water.

Opposite Bonne-Biche was a little stool for Beau-Minon while before him was a little porringer in gold, filled with little fried fish and the thighs of snipes. At one side was a bowl of rich crystal full of fresh milk.

Between Beau-Minon and Bonne-Biche a plate was placed for Blondine. Her chair was of carved ivory covered with crimson velvet attached with nails of diamonds. Before her was a gold plate richly chased, filled with delicious soup made of a young pullet and fig-birds, her glass and water-bottle were of carved rock-crystal, a muffin was placed by her side, her fork and spoon were of gold and her napkin was of linen, finer than anything she had ever seen.

The table was served by gazelles who were marvellously adroit. They waited, carved and even divined the wishes of Blondine, Bonne-Biche and Beau-Minon. The dinner was exquisite—the chicken was splendid, the game and fish most delicate, the pastry and bonbons superlative. Blondine was hungry so she ate of all and found all excellent.

After dinner, Bonne-Biche and Beau-Minon conducted the princess into the garden. She found there the most delicious fruits and lovely walks.

After a charming walk, Blondine entered the castle with her new friends, much fatigued. Bonne-Biche proposed that she retire, to which she agreed joyfully.

Blondine entered her chamber and found two gazelles waiting to attend her. They disrobed her with grace and adroitness, placed her in bed and seated themselves by her couch to watch over her.

Blondine was soon peacefully asleep—not, however, without having first thought of her father and wept bitterly over her cruel separation from him.

BLONDINE'S SECOND AWAKENING

BLONDINE slept profoundly, and on awaking she found herself entirely changed. Indeed, it seemed to her she could not be the same person. She was much taller, her intellect was developed, her knowledge enlarged. She remembered a number of books she thought she had read during her sleep. She was sure she had been writing, drawing, singing and playing on the piano and harp.

She looked around, however, and knew that the chamber was the same to which Bonne-Biche had conducted her and in which she had gone to sleep.

Agitated, disquieted, she rose and ran to the glass. She saw that she was much grown and she found herself charming, a hundred times more beautiful than when she retired the night before. Her fair ringlets fell to her feet, her complexion was like the lily and the rose, her eyes celestial blue, her nose beautifully formed, her cheeks rosy as the morn, and her form was erect and graceful. In short, Blondine thought herself the most beautiful person she had ever seen.

Trembling, almost frightened, she dressed herself hastily and ran to seek Bonne-Biche whom she found in the apartment where she had first seen her.

"Bonne-Biche, Bonne-Biche!" she exclaimed, "I entreat you to explain to me the change which I see and feel in myself. Last night I went to sleep a child—I awoke this morning, and found myself a young lady. Is this an illusion or have I indeed grown and developed thus during the night?"

"Yes, my dear Blondine, you are fourteen years old today. But you have slept peacefully seven years. My son Beau-Minon and I wished to spare you the weariness of all early studies. When you first entered the castle you knew nothing; not even how to read. I put you to sleep for seven years, and Beau-Minon and I have passed this time in instructing you during your sleep. I see by the wonder expressed in your eyes, sweet princess, that you doubt all this. Come into your study and reassure yourself on this point."

Blondine followed Bonne-Biche to the little room. She ran first to the piano, commenced playing and found that she played remarkably well. She then tried the harp and

SHE THREW HER ARMS AROUND THE NECK OF BONNE-BICHE

—Page 35

drew from it the most ravishing sounds, and she sang enchantingly.

She took her pencil and brushes and drew and painted with a facility which denoted a true talent. She wrote and found her handwriting clear and elegant. She looked at the countless books which were ranged round the room and knew that she had read them all.

Surprised, delighted, she threw her arms around the neck of Bonne-Biche, embraced Beau-Minon tenderly and said to them:

"Oh! my dear true good friends, what a debt of gratitude do I owe you for having thus watched over my childhood and developed my intellect and my heart. I feel how much I am improved in every respect and I owe it all to you."

Bonne-Biche returned her caresses and Beau-Minon patted her hand delicately. After the first few happy moments had passed, Blondine cast down her eyes and said timidly:

"Do not think me ungrateful, my dear good friends, if I wish you to add one more to the benefits you have already conferred upon me. Tell me something of my father. Does he still weep my absence? Is he happy since he lost me?"

"Dear Blondine, your anxiety on this point is most natural and shall be relieved. Look in this mirror, Blondine, and you shall see the king your father and all that has passed since you left the palace."

Blondine raised her eyes to the mirror and looked into the apartment of her father. The king seemed much agitated and was walking backwards and forwards. He appeared to be expecting some one. The queen, Fourbette, entered and related to him that notwithstanding the remonstrances of Gourmandinet, Blondine had herself seized the reins and guided the ostriches who becoming frightened dashed off in the direction of the Forest of Lilacs and overturned the carriage. Blondine was thrown over the grating which bounded the forest. She stated that Gourmandinet had become insane from terror and grief and she had sent him home to his parents. The king was in wild despair at this news. He ran to the Forest of Lilacs and he had to be withheld by force from throwing himself across the boundary in order to search for his cherished Blondine. They carried him to the palace where he yielded to the most frightful sorrow and despair, calling unceasingly upon his dear Blondine, his beloved child. At last, overcome by grief, he slept and saw in a dream Blondine in the castle of Bonne-Biche and Beau-Minon. Bonne-Biche gave him the sweet assurance that Blondine should one day be restored to him and that her childhood should be calm and happy.

The mirror now became misty and everything disappeared, then again clear as crystal and Blondine saw her father a second time. He had become old, his hair was white as snow and his countenance was sad. He held in his hand a little portrait of Blondine, his tears fell upon it and he pressed it often to his lips. The king was alone. Blondine saw neither the queen nor Brunette.

Poor Blondine wept bitterly.

"Alas!" said she, "why is my dear father alone? Where is the queen? Where is Brunette?"

"The queen," said Bonne-Biche, "showed so little grief at your death, my princess, that your father's heart was filled with hatred and suspicion towards her and he sent her back to the king Turbulent, her father, who confined her in a tower, where she soon died of rage and anger. All the world supposed you to be dead. As to your sister Brunette, she became so wicked, so insupportable, that the king hastened to give her in marriage last year to the prince Violent, who charged himself with the duty of reforming the character of the cruel and envious princess Brunette. The prince was stern and harsh. Brunette saw that her wicked heart prevented her from being happy and she commenced trying to correct her faults. You will see her again some day, dear Blondine and your example may complete her reformation."

Blondine thanked Bonne-Biche tenderly for all these details. Her heart prompted her to ask, "But when shall I see my father and sister?" But she feared to appear ungrateful and too anxious to leave the castle of her good friends. She resolved then to await another more suitable opportunity to ask this question.

The days passed away quietly and pleasantly. Blondine was much occupied, but was sometimes melancholy. She had no one to talk with but Bonne-Biche and she was only with her during the hours of lessons and repasts. Beau-Minon could not converse and could only make himself understood by signs. The gazelles served Blondine with zeal and intelligence but they had not the gift of speech.

Blondine walked every day, always accompanied by Beau-Minon, who pointed out to her the most lovely and sequestered paths and the rarest and richest flowers.

Bonne-Biche had made Blondine promise solemnly never to leave the enclosure of the park and never to enter the forest. Many times Blondine had asked Bonne-Biche the reason of this prohibition. Sighing profoundly, she had replied:

"Ah, Blondine! do not seek to penetrate the forest. It is a fatal spot. May you never enter there."

Sometimes Blondine mounted a pavilion which was built on an eminence near the boundary of the forest. She looked admiringly and longingly at the magnificent trees, the lovely and fragrant flowers, the thousand graceful birds flying and singing and seeming to call her name.

"Alas!" said she, "why will not Bonne-Biche allow me to walk in this beautiful forest? What possible danger can

I encounter in that lovely place and under her protection?"

Whenever she was lost in these reflections, Beau-Minon, who seemed to comprehend what was passing in her heart, mewed plaintively, pulled her robe and tried to draw her from the pavilion.

Blondine smiled sweetly, followed her gentle companion and recommenced her walk in the solitary park.

THE PARROT

SIX months had passed since Blondine awaked from her seven years' sleep. It seemed to the little princess a long time. The remembrance of her dear father often saddened her heart.

Bonne-Biche and Beau-Minon seemed to divine her thoughts. Beau-Minon mewed plaintively, and Bonne-Biche heaved the most profound sighs. Blondine spoke but rarely of that which occupied her thoughts continually. She feared to offend Bonne-Biche, who had said to her three or four times:

"Dear Blondine, be patient. You will see your father when you are fifteen, if you continue wise and good. Trust me, dear child; do not trouble yourself about the future and above all do not seek to leave us."

One morning Blondine was alone and very sad. She was musing upon her singular and monotonous existence. Suddenly she was disturbed in her reverie by three soft little strokes upon her window. Raising her head, she perceived a parrot with beautiful green plumage and throat and breast of bright orange.

Surprised at the appearance of a bird entirely unknown to her, she opened the window and invited the parrot to enter.

What was her amazement when the bird said to her, in a fine sharp voice:

"Good day, Blondine! I know that you sometimes have a very tedious time of it, because you have no one to talk to. I have taken pity upon you and come to have a chat with you. But I pray you do not mention that you have seen me, for Bonne-Biche would cut my throat if she knew it."

"Why so, beautiful Parrot? Bonne-Biche is good; she injures no one and only hates the wicked."

"Blondine, listen! If you do not promise to conceal my visit from Bonne-Biche and Beau-Minon, I will fly away at once and never return."

"Since you wish it so much, beautiful Parrot, I will promise silence. Let us chat a little. It is a long time since I have had an opportunity to converse. You seem to me gay and witty. I do not doubt that you will amuse me much."

Blondine listened with delight to the lively talk of the

Parrot, who complimented extravagantly her beauty, her wit and her talents.

Blondine was enchanted. In about an hour the Parrot flew away, promising to return the next day. In short, he returned every day and continued to compliment and amuse her.

One morning he struck upon the window and said:

"Blondine! Blondine! open the window, quickly! I bring you news of your father. But above all make no noise unless you want my throat cut."

Blondine was overwhelmed with joy. She opened the window with alacrity and said: "Is it true, my beautiful Parrot, that you bring me news of my dear father? Speak quickly! What is he doing and how is he?"

"Your father is well, Blondine, but he weeps your loss always. I have promised him to employ all my power to deliver you from your prison but I can do nothing without your assistance."

"My prison!" said Blondine. "But you are ignorant of all the goodness which Bonne-Biche and Beau-Minon have shown me, of the pains they have lavished upon my education, of all their tenderness and forbearance. They will be enchanted to find a way of restoring me to my father. Come with me, beautiful Parrot and I will present you to Bonne-Biche. Come, I entreat you."

"Ah! Blondine," said the sharp voice of the Parrot, "it

is you, Princess, who do not know Bonne-Biche and Beau-Minon. They detest me because I have sometimes succeeded in rescuing their victims from them. You will never see your father again, Blondine, you will never leave this forest, unless you yourself shall break the charm which holds you here."

"What charm?" said Blondine. "I know of no charm and what interest have Bonne-Biche and Beau-Minon in keeping me a prisoner?"

"Is it not to their interest to enliven their solitude, Blondine? There is a talisman which can procure your release. It is a simple Rose, which, gathered by yourself, will deliver you from your exile and restore you to the arms of your fond father."

"But there is not a single Rose in the garden. How then can I gather one?"

"I will explain this to you another day, Blondine. Now I can tell you no more, as I hear Bonne-Biche coming. But to convince you of the virtues of the Rose, entreat Bonne-Biche to give you one and see what she will say. To-morrow—to-morrow, Blondine!"

The Parrot flew away, well content to have scattered in Blondine's heart the first seeds of discontent and ingratitude.

The Parrot had scarcely disappeared when Bonne-Biche entered. She appeared greatly agitated.

"With whom have you been talking, Blondine?" looking suspiciously towards the open window.

"With no one, madam," said the princess.

"I am certain I heard voices in conversation."

"I must have been speaking to myself."

Bonne-Biche made no reply. She was very sad and tears fell from her eyes.

Blondine was also engaged in thought. The cunning words of the Parrot made her look upon the kindness of Bonne-Biche and Beau-Minon in a totally different light.

In place of saying to herself that a hind which had the power to speak, to make wild beasts intelligent, to put an infant to sleep for seven years, to dedicate seven years to a tiresome and ignorant little girl, in short, a hind lodged and served like a queen, could be no ordinary criminal; in place of cherishing a sentiment of gratitude for all that Bonne-Biche had done for her, Blondine, alas! believed blindly in the Parrot, the unknown bird of whose character and veracity she had no proof. She did not remember that the Parrot could have no possible motive for risking its life to render her a service. Blondine believed it though, implicitly, because of the flattery which the Parrot had lavished upon her. She did not even recall with gratitude the sweet and happy existence which Bonne-Biche and Beau-Minon had secured to her. She resolved to follow implicitly the counsels of the Parrot. During the course of the day she said to Bonne-Biche:—

"Why, madam, do I not see among your flowers the most lovely and charming of all flowers—the fragrant Rose?"

Bonne-Biche was greatly agitated and said in a trembling voice:—

"Blondine! Blondine! do not ask for this most perfidious flower, which pierces all who touch it! Never speak to me of the Rose, Blondine. You cannot know what fatal danger this flower contains for you!"

The expression of Bonne-Biche was so stern and severe that Blondine dared not question her further.

The day passed away sadly enough. Bonne-Biche was unhappy and Beau-Minon very sad.

Early in the morning, Blondine ran to her window and the Parrot entered the moment she opened it.

"Well, my dear Blondine, did you notice the agitation of Bonne-Biche, when you mentioned the Rose? I promised you to point out the means by which you could obtain one of these charming flowers. Listen now to my counsel. You will leave this park and enter the forest. I will accompany you and I will conduct you to a garden where you will find the most beautiful Rose in the world!"

"But how is it possible for me to leave the park? Beau-Minon always accompanies me in my walks."

"Try to get rid of him," said the Parrot; "but if that is impossible, go in spite of him."

"If this Rose is at a distance, will not my absence be perceived?"

"It is about an hour's walk. Bonne-Biche has been careful to separate you as far as possible from the Rose in order that you might not find the means to escape from her power."

"But why does she wish to hold me captive? She is all-powerful and could surely find pleasures more acceptable than educating an ignorant child."

"All this will be explained to you in the future, Blondine, when you will be in the arms of your father. Be firm! After breakfast, in some way get away from Beau-Minon and enter the forest. I will expect you there."

Blondine promised, and closed the window, fearing that Bonne-Biche would surprise her.

After breakfast, according to her usual custom, she entered the garden. Beau-Minon followed her in spite of some rude rebuffs which he received with plaintive mews. Arrived at the alley which led out of the park, Blondine resolved to get rid of Beau-Minon.

"I wish to be alone," said she, sternly; "begone, Beau-Minon!"

Beau-Minon pretended not to understand. Blondine was impatient and enraged. She forgot herself so far as to strike Beau-Minon with her foot. When poor Beau-Minon received this humiliating blow, he uttered a cry of anguish and fled towards the palace. Blondine trembled and was on the point of recalling him, when a false shame arrested her. She walked on rapidly to the gate, opened it not without trembling and entered the forest. The Parrot joined her without delay.

"Courage, Blondine! in one hour you will have the Rose and will see your father, who weeps for you."

At these words, Blondine recovered her resolution which had begun to falter. She walked on in the path indicated by the Parrot, who flew before her from branch to branch. The forest, which had seemed so beautiful and attractive near the park of Bonne-Biche, became wilder and more entangled. Brambles and stones almost filled up the path, the sweet songs of the birds were no longer heard and the flowers had entirely disappeared. Blondine felt oppressed by an inexplicable restlessness. The Parrot pressed her eagerly to advance.

"Quick, quick, Blondine! time flies! If Bonne-Biche perceives your absence you will never again see your father."

Blondine, fatigued, almost breathless, with her arms torn by the briers and her shoes in shreds, now declared that she would go no further when the Parrot exclaimed:—

"We have arrived, Blondine. Look! that is the enclosure which separates us from the Rose."

Blondine saw at a turn in the path a small enclosure, the gate of which was quickly opened by the Parrot. The soil was arid and stony but a magnificent, majestic rose-bush adorned with one Rose, which was more beautiful than all the roses of the world grew in the midst of this sterile spot.

"Take it, Blondine!" said the parrot; "you deserve it—you have truly earned it!"

Blondine seized the branch eagerly and in spite of the thorns which pierced her fingers cruelly, she tore it from the bush.

The Rose was scarcely grasped firmly in her hand, when she heard a burst of mocking laughter. The Flower fell from her grasp, crying:—

"Thanks, Blondine, for having delivered me from the prison in which Bonne-Biche held me captive. I am your evil genius! Now you belong to me!"

"Ha! ha!" now exclaimed the Parrot. "Thanks, Blondine! I can now resume my form of magician. You have destroyed your friends for I am their mortal enemy!"

Saying these cruel words, the Parrot and the Rose disappeared, leaving Blondine alone in the forest.

REPENTANCE

BLONDINE was stupefied! Her conduct now appeared to her in all its horror. She had shown a monstrous ingratitude towards the friends who had been so tenderly devoted to her—who had dedicated seven years to the care of her education. Would these kind friends ever receive her, ever pardon her? What would be her fate, if they should close their doors against her? And then, what did those awful words of the wicked Parrot signify: "You have caused the destruction of your friends"?

Blondine turned round and wished to retrace her steps to the castle of Bonne-Biche. The briers and thorns tore her arms and face terribly. She continued however to force her way bravely through the thickets and after three hours of most painful walking she came before the castle of Bonne-Biche and Beau-Minon.

Horror seized upon her, when in place of the superb building she saw only an appalling ruin—in place of the magnificent trees and rare flowers which surrounded it, only briers and thorns, nettles and thistles, could be seen. Terrified and most desolate, she tried to force her way in the midst of the ruins, to seek some knowledge of her kind

Blondine sees the castle of Bonne-Biche and Beau-Minon

friends. A large Toad issued from a pile of stones, advanced before her, and said:—

"What are you seeking? Have you not occasioned the death of your friends by the basest ingratitude? Begone! do not insult their memory by your unwelcome presence!"

"Alas! alas!" cried Blondine, "my poor friends, Bonne-Biche and Beau-Minon, why can I not atone by my death for the sufferings I have caused them?" And she fell, sobbing piteously, upon the stones and nettles; her grief and her repentance were so excessive that she did not feel their sharp points in her tender flesh. She wept profusely a long time. At last she arose and looked about her, hoping to find some shelter where she might take refuge. Ruin only stared her in the face!

"Well," said she, "let the wild beasts tear me to pieces, let me die of hunger and thirst, if I can expiate my sins here upon the tomb of Bonne-Biche and Beau-Minon!"

As she uttered these words, she heard a soft voice saying: "True repentance can atone for the worst of crimes."

She raised her head and saw only an immense black Crow flying above her.

"Alas! alas!" said Blondine, "my repentance however true, however bitter it may be, can never give me back the lives of my dear Bonne-Biche and Beau-Minon!"

"Courage, courage, Blondine! redeem your fault by

your repentance and do not allow yourself to be utterly cast down by grief."

The poor princess arose and left the scene of desolation. She followed a little path, where the large trees seemed to have rooted out the brambles and the earth was covered with moss. She was utterly exhausted with grief and fatigue and fell at the foot of a large tree, sobbing piteously.

"Courage, Blondine!" said another voice; "courage and hope!"

She saw near her only a Frog, which was looking at her compassionately.

"Oh, Frog!" said the princess, "you seem to pity my anguish! What will become of me now that I am alone and desolate in the world?"

"Courage and hope!" was the reply.

Blondine sighed deeply and looked around, hoping to discover some herb or fruit to appease her hunger and thirst. She saw nothing and her tears flowed freely. The sound of bells now somewhat dissipated her despairing thoughts. She saw a beautiful cow approaching her, gently and slowly. On arriving near her, the cow paused, bowed down, and showed her a silver porringer attached to her neck by a chain of beaten gold.

Blondine was very grateful for this unexpected succor. She detached the porringer, milked the cow and drank the sweet milk with delight. The pretty, gentle cow signed to her to replace the porringer. Blondine obeyed, kissed her on the neck and said, sadly:—

"Thanks, Blanchette, it is without doubt to my poor friends that I owe this sweet charity. Perhaps in another and better world they can see the repentance of their poor Blondine and wish to assist her in her frightful position."

"A true repentance will obtain pardon for all faults," said a kind voice.

"Ah!" exclaimed Blondine, "years of sorrow and weeping for my crimes would not suffice! I can never pardon myself!"

In the mean time, night approached. Notwithstanding her anguish and repentance, Blondine began to reflect upon some means of securing herself from the ferocious wild beasts, whose terrible roars she already believed she heard in the distance. She saw some steps before her a kind of hut, formed by several trees growing near together and interlacing their branches. Bowing her head, she entered, and found that by carefully connecting some branches she could form a pretty and secure retreat. She employed the remainder of the day in arranging this little room and gathered a quantity of moss, with which she made herself a bed and pillow. She concealed the entrance to this little retreat by some broken branches and leaves and went to rest, utterly worn out with regret and fatigue.

When Blondine awoke it was broad daylight. At first

she could scarcely collect her thoughts and understand her position but the sad realities of her lot were soon apparent to her and she commenced weeping as before.

Blondine was hungry, and she could not imagine how she was to secure food but soon she heard again the sound of the cow-bells. In a few moments, Blanchette stood near her. Blondine again loosened the porringer, drew the milk and drank till her hunger was appeased, then replaced the porringer and kissed Blanchette, hoping to see her again during the day. Every day—in the morning, at midday and in the evening—Blanchette came to offer Blondine her frugal repast.

Blondine passed the time in tears for her poor friends, and bitter self-reproach for her crimes.

"By my unpardonable disobedience," she said to herself, "I have caused the most terrible misfortunes, which it is not in my power to repair. I have not only lost my good and true friends but I am deprived of the only means of finding my father, my poor father, who perhaps still expects his Blondine, his most unhappy Blondine, condemned to live and die alone in this frightful forest where her evil genius reigns supreme."

Blondine sought to amuse and employ herself in every possible way. Her little home was neatly arranged, and fresh moss and leaves composed her simple couch. She had tied some branches together and formed a seat and she made herself some needles and pins of the thorns and twisted some thread from the hemp which grew near her little hut, and with these implements she had mended the rents in her shoes.

In this simple way Blondine lived for six months; her grief was always the same and it is just to say that it was not her sad and solitary life which made her unhappy but sincere regret for her fault. She would willingly have consented to pass her life in the forest if she could thus have brought to life Bonne-Biche and Beau-Minon.

THE TORTOISE

ONE day Blondine was seated at the entrance of her hut, musing sadly as usual, thinking of her lost friends and of her father, when she saw before her an enormous Tortoise.

"Blondine," said the Tortoise, "if you will place yourself under my protection, I will conduct you out of this forest."

"And why, Madam Tortoise, should I seek to leave this forest? Here I caused the death of my friends and here I wish to die."

"Are you very certain of their death, Blondine?"

"What do you mean? Is it possible I may be deceived? But, no; I saw the ruins of their castle. The Parrot and the Toad assured me of their death. You are kind and good and wish to console me without doubt but, alas! I do not hope to see them again. If they still lived they would not have left me alone with the frightful despair of having caused their death."

"But how do you know, Blondine, that this seeming neglect is not forced upon them? They may now be subjected to a power greater than their own. You know, Blondine, that a true repentance will obtain pardon for many crimes."

"Ah! Madam Tortoise, if they still live, if you can give me news of them, if you can assure me that I need no longer reproach myself with their death, assure me that I shall one day see them again, there is no price which I will not gladly pay to merit this great happiness."

"Blondine, I am not permitted to disclose to you the fate of your friends but if you have the courage to mount on my back, remain there for six months and not address a single question to me during the journey, I will conduct you to a place where all will be revealed."

"I promise all that you ask, Madam Tortoise, provided I can only learn what has become of my friends."

"Take care, Blondine! reflect well. Six months without descending from my back and without asking me a single question! When once you have accepted the conditions, when we have commenced our journey, if you have not the courage to endure to the end, you will remain eternally in the power of the enchanter, Perroquet, and his sister Rose and I cannot even continue to bestow upon you the little assistance to which you owe your life during the last six months."

"Let us go, Madam Tortoise let us be off, immediately. I prefer to die of hunger and fatigue rather than of grief and uncertainty. Your words have brought hope to my poor heart, and I have courage to undertake even a more difficult journey than that of which you speak."

"Let it be according to your wish, Blondine. Mount my back. Fear neither hunger nor thirst nor cold nor sunshine nor any accident during our long journey. As long as it lasts you shall not suffer from any inconvenience."

Blondine mounted on the back of the Tortoise. "Now, silence!" said she; "and not one word till we have arrived and I speak to you first."

THE JOURNEY AND ARRIVAL

THE journey of Blondine lasted, as the Tortoise had said, six months. They were three months passing through the forest. At the end of that time she found herself on an arid plain which it required six weeks to cross. Then Blondine perceived a castle which reminded her of that of Bonne-Biche and Beau-Minon. They were a full month passing through the avenue to this castle.

Blondine burned with impatience. Would she indeed learn the fate of her dear friends at the palace? In spite of her extreme anxiety, she dared not ask a single question. If she could have descended from the back of the Tortoise, ten minutes would have sufficed for her to reach the castle. But, alas! the Tortoise crept on slowly and Blondine remembered that she had been forbidden to alight or to utter a word. She resolved, therefore, to control her impatience. The Tortoise seemed rather to relax than to increase her speed. She consumed fourteen days still in passing through this avenue. They seemed fourteen centuries to Blondine. She never, however, lost sight of the castle or of the door. The place seemed deserted; she heard no noise, she saw no sign of life.

At last, after twenty-four days' journey, the Tortoise paused, and said to Blondine:—

"Now, princess, descend. By your courage and obedience you have earned the recompense I promised. Enter the little door which you see before you. The first person you will meet will be the fairy Bienveillante and she will make known to you the fate of your friends."

Blondine sprang lightly to the earth. She had been immovable so long she feared her limbs would be cramped but on the contrary she was as light and active as when she had lived so happily with her dear Bonne-Biche and Beau-Minon and ran joyously and gracefully gathering flowers and chasing butterflies.

After having thanked the Tortoise most warmly she opened the door which had been pointed out to her and found herself before a young person clothed in white, who asked in a sweet voice, whom she desired to see?

"I wish to see the fairy Bienveillante. Tell her, I pray

THEY WERE THREE MONTHS PASSING THROUGH THE FOREST

—*Page 59*

you, miss, that the princess Blondine begs earnestly to see her without delay."

"Follow me, princess," replied the young girl.

Blondine followed in great agitation. She passed through several beautiful rooms and met many young girls clothed in white, like her guide. They looked at her as if they recognized her and smiled graciously.

At last Blondine arrived in a room in every respect resembling that of Bonne-Biche in the Forest of Lilacs. The remembrances which this recalled were so painful that she did not perceive the disappearance of her fair young guide.

Blondine gazed sadly at the furniture of the room. She saw but one piece which had not adorned the apartment of Bonne-Biche in the Forest of Lilacs. This was a wardrobe in gold and ivory, exquisitely carved. It was closed. Blondine felt herself drawn towards it in an inexplicable manner. She was gazing at it intently, not having indeed the power to turn her eyes away, when a door opened and a young and beautiful woman, magnificently dressed, entered and drew near Blondine.

"What do you wish, my child?" said she, in a sweet, caressing voice.

"Oh, madam!" said Blondine, throwing herself at her feet, "I have been assured that you could give me news of my dear, kind friends, Bonne-Biche and Beau-Minon. You know, madam, without doubt by what heedless disobedience I gave them up to destruction and that I wept for them a long time, believing them to be dead but the Tortoise, who conducted me here, has given me reason to hope I may one day see them again. Tell me, madam, tell me if they yet live and if I may dare hope for the happiness of rejoining them?"

"Blondine," replied the fairy Bienveillante, sadly, "you are now about to know the fate of your friends, but no matter what you see or hear, do not lose courage or hope."

Saying these words, she seized the trembling Blondine and conducted her in front of the wardrobe which had already so forcibly attracted her attention.

"Blondine, here is the key to this wardrobe. Open it, and be brave!"

She handed Blondine a gold key. With a trembling hand the princess opened the wardrobe. What was her anguish when she saw the skins of Bonne-Biche and Beau-Minon fastened to the wardrobe with diamond nails! At this terrible sight the unfortunate princess uttered a cry of horror and fell insensible at the feet of the fairy. At this moment the door opened and a prince, beautiful as the day, sprang towards Blondine, saying:—

"Oh, my mother! this is too severe a trial for my sweet Blondine!"

"Alas! my son, my heart also bleeds for her. But you know that this last punishment was indispensable to deliver her for ever from the yoke of the cruel genius of the Forest of Lilacs."

The fairy Bienveillante now with her wand touched Blondine, who was immediately restored to consciousness but despairing and sobbing convulsively, she exclaimed:—

"Let me die at once! My life is odious to me! No hope, no happiness, from this time forth for ever for poor Blondine! My friends! my cherished friends! I will join you soon in the land of shadows!"

"Blondine! ever dear Blondine!" said the fairy, clasping her in her arms, "your friends live and love you tenderly. I am Bonne-Biche and this is my son, Beau-Minon. The wicked genius of the Forest of Lilacs, taking advantage of the negligence of my son, obtained dominion over us and forced us into the forms under which you have known us. We could not resume our natural appearance unless you should pluck the Rose, which I, knowing it to be your evil genius, retained captive. I placed it as far as possible from the castle in order to withdraw it from your view. I knew the misfortune to which you would be exposed on delivering your evil genius from his prison and Heaven is my witness, that my son and I would willingly have remained a Hind and a Cat for ever in your eyes in order to spare you the cruel tortures to which you have been subjected. The Parrot gained you over, in spite of all our precautions. You know the rest, my dear child. But you can never know all that we have suffered in witnessing your tears and your desolation."

Blondine embraced the Fairy ardently and addressed a thousand questions to her.

"What has become of the gazelles who waited upon us so gracefully?"

"You have already seen them, dear Blondine. They are the young girls who accompanied you. They also were changed when the evil genius gained his power over us."

"And the good white cow who brought me milk every day?"

"We obtained permission from the Queen of the Fairies to send you this light refreshment. The encouraging words of the Crow came also from us."

"You, then, madam, also sent me the Tortoise?"

"Yes, Blondine. The Queen of the Fairies, touched by your repentance and your grief, deprived the Evil Genius of the Forest of all power over us on condition of obtaining from you one last proof of submission, compelling you to take this long and fatiguing journey and inflicting the terrible punishment of making you believe that my son and I had died from your imprudence. I implored, entreated the Queen of the Fairies to spare you at least this last anguish but she was inflexible."

Blondine gazed at her lost friends, listened eagerly to every word and did not cease to embrace those she had feared were eternally separated from her by death. The remembrance of her dear father now presented itself. The prince Parfait understood her secret desire and made it known to his mother, the fairy Bienveillante.

"Prepare yourself, dear Blondine, to see your father. Informed by me, he now expects you."

At this moment, Blondine found herself in a chariot of gold and pearls, the fairy Bienveillante seated at her right hand, and the prince Parfait at her feet, regarding her kindly and tenderly. The chariot was drawn by four swans of dazzling whiteness. They flew with such rapidity, that five minutes brought them to the palace of King Benin. All the court was assembled about the king, all were expecting the princess Blondine.

When the chariot appeared, the cries of joy and welcome were so tumultuous that the swans were confused and almost lost their way. Prince Parfait, who guided them, succeeded in arresting their attention and the chariot drew up at the foot of the grand stairway. King Benin sprang towards Blondine who, jumping lightly from the chariot, threw herself in her father's arms. They remained a long time in this position and everybody wept tears of joy.

When King Benin had somewhat recovered himself he kissed, respectfully and tenderly, the hand of the good fairy who, after having protected and educated the princess Blondine had now restored her to him. He embraced the prince Parfait whom he found most charming.

There were eight resplendent gala days in honor of the return of Blondine. At the close of this gay festival, the fairy Bienveillante announced her intention of returning home. But Prince Parfait and Blondine were so melancholy at the prospect of this separation that King Benin resolved they should never quit the place. He wedded the fairy and Blondine became the happy wife of Prince Parfait who was always for her the Beau-Minon of the Forest of Lilacs.

Brunette, whose character had entirely changed, came often to see Blondine. Prince Violent, her husband, became more amiable as Brunette became more gentle and they were very happy.

As to Blondine, she had no misfortunes, no griefs. She had lovely daughters, who resembled her, and good and handsome sons, the image of their manly father, Prince Parfait. Everybody loved them and every one connected with them was happy ever after.

Good Little Henry

GOOD LITTLE HENRY

THE POOR SICK MOTHER

THERE was a poor woman, a widow, who lived alone with her little son Henry. She loved him tenderly and she had good reason to do so, for no one had ever seen a more charming child. Although he was but seven years old, he kept the house while his good mother labored diligently and then left home to sell her work and buy food for herself and her little Henry. He swept, he washed the floor, he cooked, he dug and cultivated the garden and when all this was done he seated himself to mend his clothes or his mother's shoes and to make stools and tables—in short, to do everything his strength would enable him to do.

The house in which they lived belonged to them, but it was very lonesome. In front of their dwelling there was a lofty mountain so high that no one had ever ascended to its summit, and besides it was surrounded by a rushing torrent, by high walls and insurmountable precipices.

The mother and her little boy were happy but alas! one day the poor mother fell sick. They knew no doctor and besides they had no money to pay for one. Poor Henry did not know how to cure her. He brought her fresh cool water for he had nothing else to give her, he stayed by her night and day and ate his little morsel of dry bread at the foot of her bed. When she slept he looked at her sadly and wept. The sickness increased from day to day and at last the poor woman was almost in a dying condition. She could neither speak nor swallow and she no longer knew her little Henry, who was sobbing on his knees near her bed. In his despair, he cried out:

"Fairy Bienfaisante, come to my help! Save my mother!"

Henry had scarcely pronounced these words, when a window opened and a lady richly dressed entered and in a soft voice, said to him:

"What do you wish of me, my little friend? You called me—here I am!"

"Madam," cried Henry, throwing himself on his knees and clasping his hands, "if you are the fairy Bienfaisante, save my poor mother who is about to die and leave me alone in the world."

The good fairy looked at Henry most compassionately and then, without saying a word, she approached the poor woman, bent over her, examined her attentively, breathed upon her and said:

"It is not in my power, my poor child, to cure your mother; her life depends upon you alone, if you have the courage to undertake the journey I will point out to you."

"Speak, madam! I entreat you to speak! there is nothing I will not undertake to save the life of my dear mother."

The fairy replied,

"You must go and seek the plant of life, which grows on top of the mountain that you see from this window. When you have obtained this plant, press its juice into the mouth of your mother and she will be immediately restored to health."

"I will start out immediately, madam. But who will take care of my poor mother during my absence? And, moreover," said he, sobbing bitterly, "she will be dead before my return."

"Do not worry, my dear child. If you go to seek the plant of life, your mother will need nothing before your return; she will remain precisely in the condition in which you leave her. But you must dare many dangers and endure many things before you pluck the plant of life. Great courage and great perseverance are necessary on your part."

"I fear nothing, madam, my courage and perseverance shall not fail. Tell me only how I shall know this plant amongst all the others which cover the top of the mountain."

"When you reach the summit, call the doctor who has charge of this plant, inform him that I have sent you and he will give you a branch of the plant of life."

Henry kissed the good fairy's hands and thanked her heartily, took a sorrowful leave of his mother, covering her with kisses, put some bread in his pocket and set out, after saluting the fairy respectfully.

The fairy smiled encouragingly at this poor child who so bravely resolved to ascend a mountain so dangerous that none of those who had attempted it had ever reached the summit.

THE CROW, THE COCK, AND THE FROG

LITTLE HENRY marched resolutely to the mountain which he found much more distant than it had appeared to him. Instead of arriving in a half hour as he had expected, he walked rapidly the whole day without reaching its base.

About one-third of the way he saw a Crow which was caught by the claw in a snare which some wicked boy had set for him. The poor Crow sought in vain to release himself from this trap which caused him cruel sufferings. Henry ran to him, cut the cord which bound him and set him at liberty. The poor Crow flew off rapidly, after having said to Henry,

"Thanks, my brave Henry, I will see you again."

Henry was much surprised to hear the Crow speak but he did not relax his speed.

Some time afterwards while he was resting in a grove and eating a morsel of bread, he saw a Cock followed by a fox and about to be taken by him in spite of his efforts to escape. The poor frightened Cock passed very near to Henry, who seized it adroitly, and hid it under his coat without the fox having seen him. The fox continued his pursuit, supposing that the Cock was before him. Henry did not move till he was entirely out of sight. He then released the Cock, who said to him in a low voice:

"Many thanks, my brave Henry, I will see you again."

Henry was now rested. He rose and continued his journey. When he had advanced a considerable distance he saw a poor Frog about to be devoured by a serpent. The Frog trembled and, paralyzed by fear, could not move. The serpent advanced rapidly, its horrid mouth open. Henry seized a large stone and threw it so adroitly that it entered the serpent's throat the moment it was about to devour the Frog. The frightened Frog leaped to a distance and cried out,

"Many thanks, brave Henry; we will meet again."

Henry, who had before heard the Crow and the Cock speak, was not now astonished at these words of the Frog and continued to walk on rapidly.

A short time after he arrived at the foot of the mountain but he was greatly distressed to see that a large and deep river ran at its foot, so wide that the other side could scarcely be seen. Greatly at a loss he paused to reflect.

A large and deep river ran at the foot of the mountain

"Perhaps," said he, hopefully, "I may find a bridge, or ford, or a boat."

Henry followed the course of the river which flowed entirely around the mountain but everywhere it was equally wide and deep and he saw neither bridge nor boat. Poor Henry seated himself on the bank of the river, weeping bitterly.

"Fairy Bienfaisante! Fairy Bienfaisante! come to my

help," he exclaimed. "Of what use will it be to me to know that there is a plant at the top of the mountain which will save the life of my poor mother, if I can never reach its summit?"

At this moment the Cock whom he had protected from the fox appeared on the borders of the river, and said to him:

"The fairy Bienfaisante can do nothing for you. This mountain is beyond her control. But you have saved my life and I wish to prove my gratitude. Mount my back, Henry, and by the faith of a Cock I will take you safe to the other side."

Henry did not hesitate. He sprang on the Cock's back, fully expecting to fall into the water but his clothes were not even moist. The Cock received him so adroitly on his back that he felt as secure as if he had been on horseback. He held on firmly to the crest of the Cock who now commenced the passage.

The river was so wide that he was flying constantly twenty-one days before he reached the other shore; but during these twenty-one days Henry was not sleepy and felt neither hunger nor thirst.

When they arrived, Henry thanked the Cock most politely, who graciously bristled his feathers and disappeared. A moment after this Henry turned and to his astonishment the river was no longer to be seen.

"It was without doubt the genius of the mountain who

wished to prevent my approach," said Henry. "But, with the help of the good fairy Bienfaisante, I think I shall yet succeed in my mission."

THE HARVEST

HENRY walked a long, long time but he walked in vain for he saw that he was no farther from the foot of the mountain and no nearer to the summit than he had been when he crossed the river. Any other child would have retraced his steps but the brave little Henry would not allow himself to be discouraged. Notwithstanding his extreme fatigue he walked on twenty-one days without seeming to make any advance. At the end of this time he was no more discouraged than at the close of the first day.

"If I am obliged to walk a hundred years," he said aloud, "I will go on till I reach the summit."

"You have then a great desire to arrive there, little boy?" said an old man, looking at him maliciously and standing just in his path. "What are you seeking at the top of this mountain?"

"The plant of life, my good sir, to save the life of my dear mother who is about to die."

The little old man shook his head, rested his little pointed chin on the top of his gold-headed cane and after having a long time regarded Henry, he said:

"Your sweet and fresh face pleases me, my boy. I am one of the genii of this mountain. I will allow you to advance on condition that you will gather all my wheat, that you will beat it out, make it into flour and then into bread. When you have gathered, beaten, ground and cooked it, then call me. You will find all the necessary implements in the ditch near you. The fields of wheat are before you and cover the mountain."

The old man disappeared and Henry gazed in terror at the immense fields of wheat which were spread out before him. But he soon mastered this feeling of discouragement—took off his vest, seized a scythe and commenced cutting the wheat diligently. This occupied him a hundred and ninety-five days and nights.

When the wheat was all cut, Henry commenced to beat it with a flail which he found at hand. This occupied him sixty days.

When the grain was all beaten out he began to grind it in a mill which rose up suddenly near him. This occupied him seventy days.

When the wheat was all ground he began to knead it

and to cook it. He kneaded and cooked for a hundred and twenty days.

As the bread was cooked he arranged it properly on shelves, like books in a library.

When all was finished Henry was transported with joy and called the genius of the mountain who appeared immediately and counted four hundred and sixty-eight thousand three hundred and twenty-nine new loaves of bread. He bit and ate a little end off of two or three, drew near to Henry, tapped him on the cheek and said:

"You are a good boy and I wish to pay you for your work."

He drew from his pocket a little wooden box which he gave to Henry and said, maliciously:

"When you return home, open this box and you will find in it the most delicious tobacco you have ever seen."

Now Henry had never used tobacco and the present of the little genius seemed to him very useless but he was too polite to let this be seen and he thanked the old man as if satisfied.

The old one smiled, then burst out laughing and disappeared.

THE VINTAGE

HENRY began to walk rapidly and perceived with great delight that every step brought him nearer to the summit of the mountain. In three hours he had walked two-thirds of the way. But suddenly he found himself arrested by a very high wall which he had not perceived before. He walked around it, and found, after three days' diligent advance, that this wall surrounded the entire mountain and that there was no door, not the smallest opening by which he could enter.

Henry seated himself on the ground, to reflect upon his situation. He resolved to wait patiently—he sat there forty-five days. At the end of this time he said:

"I will not go back if I have to wait here a hundred years."

He had scarcely uttered these words when a part of the

wall crumbled away with a terrible noise and he saw in the opening a giant, brandishing an enormous cudgel.

"You have then a great desire to pass here, my boy? What are you seeking beyond my wall?"

"I am seeking the plant of life, Master Giant, to cure my poor mother who is dying. If it is in your power and you will allow me to pass this wall, I will do anything for you that you may command."

"Is it so? Well, listen! Your countenance pleases me. I am one of the genii of this mountain. I will allow you to pass this wall if you will fill my wine-cellar. Here are all my vines. Gather the grapes, crush them, put the juice in the casks and arrange them well in my wine-cellar. You will find all the implements necessary at the foot of this wall. When it is done, call me."

The Giant disappeared, closing the wall behind him. Henry looked around him and as far as he could see, the vines of the Giant were growing luxuriously.

"Well, well," said Henry to himself, "I cut all the wheat of the little old man—I can surely also gather the grapes of the big Giant. It will not take me so long and it will not be as difficult to make wine of these grapes as to make bread of the wheat."

Henry took off his coat, picked up a pruning-knife which he saw at his feet and began to cut the grapes and throw them into the vats. It took him thirty days to gather

A PART OF THE WALL CRUMBLED WITH A TERRIBLE NOISE

—*Page 82*

this crop. When all was finished, he crushed the grapes, poured the juice into the casks and ranged them in the cellar, which they completely filled. He was ninety days making the wine.

When the wine was ready and everything in the cellar in complete order, Henry called the Giant who immediately appeared, examined the casks, tasted the wine, then turned towards Henry and said:

"You are a brave little man and I wish to pay you for your trouble. It shall not be said that you worked gratis for the Giant of the mountain."

He drew a thistle from his pocket, gave it to Henry and said:

"After your return home, whenever you desire anything, smell this thistle."

Henry did not think the Giant very generous but he received the thistle with an amiable smile.

Then the Giant whistled so loudly that the mountain trembled and the wall and Giant disappeared entirely and Henry was enabled to continue his journey.

THE CHASE

HENRY was within a half-hour's walk of the summit of the mountain when he reached a pit so wide that he could not possibly jump to the other side and so deep that it seemed bottomless. Henry did not lose courage, however. He followed the borders of the pit till he found himself where he started from and knew that this yawning pit surrounded the mountain.

"Alas! what shall I do?" said poor Henry; "I scarcely overcome one obstacle when another more difficult seems to rise up before me. How shall I ever pass this pit?"

The poor child felt for the first time that his eyes were filled with tears. He looked around for some means of passing over but saw no possible chance and seated himself sadly on the brink of the precipice. Suddenly he heard a terrible growl. He turned and saw within ten steps of him an enormous Wolf gazing at him with flaming eyes.

"What are you seeking in my kingdom?" said the Wolf, in a threatening voice.

"Master Wolf, I am seeking the plant of life which alone can save my dear mother who is about to die. If you will assist me to cross this pit, I will be your devoted servant and will obey any command you may give me."

"Well, my boy, if you will catch all the game which is in my forests, birds and beasts, and make them up into pies and nice roasts, by the faith of the genius of the mountain, I will pass you over to the other side. You will find near this tree all the instruments necessary to catch the game and to cook it. When your work is done, call me."

Saying these words, he disappeared.

Henry took courage. He lifted a bow and arrow which he saw on the ground, and began to shoot at the partridges, woodcocks, pheasants and game of all kinds which abounded there. But, alas! he did not understand it and killed nothing.

During eight days he was shooting right and left in vain and was at last wearied and despairing, when he saw near him the Crow whose life he had saved in the commencement of his journey.

"You rescued me from mortal danger," said the Crow, "and I told you I should see you again. I have come to redeem my promise. If you do not fulfil your promise to the Wolf, he will change you into some terrible wild beast. Follow me. I am going a-hunting and you have only to gather the game and cook it."

Saying these words, the Crow flew above the trees of the forest and with his beak and his claws killed all the game to be found. In fact, during one hundred and fifty days he caught one million eight hundred and sixty thousand seven hundred and twenty-six animals and birds, squirrels, moorcocks, pheasants, and quails. As the Crow killed them, Henry plucked the feathers, skinned them, cut them up and cooked them in roasts or pies. When all was cooked he arranged them neatly and then the Crow said to him:

"Adieu, Henry. There remains one obstacle yet to overcome but in that difficulty I cannot aid you. But do not be discouraged. The good fairies protect filial love."

Before Henry had time to thank the Crow, he had disappeared. He then called the Wolf and said to him:

"Master Wolf, here is all the game of your forest. I have prepared it as you ordered and now will you assist me to pass this precipice?"

The Wolf examined a pheasant, crunched a roast squirrel and a pie, licked his lips and said to Henry:

"You are a brave and good boy. I will pay you for your trouble. It shall not be said that you have worked for the Wolf of the mountain without receiving your reward."

Saying these words, he gave Henry a staff which he cut in the forest and said to him:

Henry sprang upon the Wolf's back

"When you have gathered the plant of life and wish yourself transported to any part of the world, mount the stick and it will be your horse."

Henry was on the point of throwing this useless stick into the woods but he wished to be polite, and receiving it smilingly, he thanked the Wolf cordially.

"Get on my back, Henry," said the Wolf.

Henry sprang upon the Wolf's back and he made a

bound so prodigious that they landed immediately on the other side of the precipice.

Henry dismounted, thanked the Wolf and walked on vigorously.

THE FISHING

AT last, after so many labors and perils, Henry saw the lattice of the garden in which the plant of life was growing and his heart bounded for joy. He looked always upward as he walked, and went on as rapidly as his strength would permit, when suddenly he fell into a hole. He sprang backwards, looked anxiously around him and saw a ditch full of water, large and long, so long indeed that he could not see either end.

"Without doubt this is that last obstacle of which the Crow spoke to me," said Henry to himself. "Since I have overcome all my other difficulties with the help of the good fairy Bienfaisante, she will assist me to surmount this also. It was surely she who sent me the Cock, the Crow and the Old Man, the Giant and the Wolf. I will wait patiently till it shall please her to assist me this time."

On saying these words, Henry began to walk along the ditch, hoping to find the end. He walked on steadily two days and found himself at the end of that time just where he had started. Henry would not give way to distress, he would not be discouraged; he seated himself on the borders of the ditch and said:

"I will not move from this spot till the genius of the mountain allows me to pass this ditch."

Henry had just uttered these words when an enormous Cat appeared before him and began to mew so horribly that he was almost deafened by the sound. The Cat said to him:

"What are you doing here? Do you not know that I could tear you to pieces with one stroke of my claws?"

"I do not doubt your power, Mr. Cat, but you will not do so when you know that I am seeking the plant of life to save my poor mother who is dying. If you will permit me to pass your ditch, I will do anything in my power to please you."

"Will you?" said the Cat. "Well, then, listen; your countenance pleases me. If, therefore, you will catch all the fish in this ditch and salt and cook them, I will pass you over to the other side, on the faith of a Cat!"

Henry advanced some steps and saw lines, fish-hooks, bait, and nets on the ground. He took a net, and hoped that by one vigorous haul he would take many fish and that he would succeed much better than with a line and hook. He threw the net and drew it in with great caution. But alas! he had caught nothing!

Disappointed, Henry thought he had not been adroit. He threw the net again and drew it very softly: still nothing!

Henry was patient. For ten days he tried faithfully without having caught a single fish. Then he gave up the net and tried the hook and line. He waited an hour, two hours;—not a single fish bit at the bait! He moved from place to place, till he had gone entirely around the ditch. He tried diligently fifteen days and caught not a single fish. He knew not now what to do. He thought of the good fairy Bienfaisante, who had abandoned him at the end of his undertaking. He seated himself sadly and gazed intently at the ditch when suddenly the water began to boil and he saw the head of a Frog appear.

"Henry," said the Frog, "you saved my life—I wish now to save yours in return. If you do not execute the orders of the Cat of the mountain he will eat you for his breakfast. You cannot catch the fish because the water is so deep and they take refuge at the bottom. But allow me to act for you. Light your fire for cooking and prepare your vessels for salting. I will bring you the fish."

Saying these words, the Frog plunged back into the water. Henry saw that the waves were agitated and boiling up, as if a grand contest was going on at the bottom of the ditch. In a moment, however, the Frog reappeared, sprang ashore and deposited a superb salmon which he had caught. Henry had scarcely time to seize the salmon when the Frog leaped ashore with a carp. During sixty days the Frog continued his labors. Henry cooked the large fish and threw the little ones into the casks to be salted. Finally, at the end of two months, the Frog leaped towards Henry and said:

"There is not now a single fish in the ditch. You can call the Cat of the mountain."

Henry thanked the Frog heartily, who extended his wet foot towards him, in sign of friendship. Henry pressed it affectionately and gratefully and the Frog disappeared.

It took Henry fifteen days to arrange properly all the large fish he had cooked and all the casks of small fish he had salted. He then called the Cat, who appeared immediately.

"Mr. Cat," said Henry, "here are all your fish cooked and salted. Will you now keep your promise and pass me over to the other side?"

The Cat examined the fish and the casks; tasted a salted and a cooked fish, licked his lips, smiled and said to Henry:

"You are a brave boy! I will recompense your fortitude and patience. It shall never be said that the Cat of the mountain does not pay his servants."

Saying these words, the Cat tore off one of his own claws and said, handing it to Henry:

"When you are sick or feel yourself growing old, touch your forehead with this claw. Sickness, suffering and old age will disappear. This miraculous claw will have the same virtue for all that you love and all who love you."

Henry thanked the Cat most warmly, took the precious claw and wished to try its powers immediately, as he felt painfully weary. The claw had scarcely touched his brow when he felt as fresh and vigorous as if he had just left his bed.

The Cat looked on smiling, and said: "Now get on my tail."

Henry obeyed. He was no sooner seated on the Cat's tail than he saw the tail lengthen itself till it reached across the ditch.

THE PLANT OF LIFE

WHEN he had saluted the Cat respectfully, Henry ran towards the garden of the plant of life, which was only a hundred steps from him. He trembled lest some new obstacle should retard him but he reached the garden lattice without any difficulty. He sought the gate and found it readily, as the garden was not large. But, alas! the garden was filled with innumerable plants utterly unknown to him and it was impossible to know how to distinguish the plant of life. Happily he remembered that the good fairy Bienfaisante had told him that when he reached the summit of the mountain he must call the Doctor who cultivated the garden of the fairies. He called him then with a loud voice. In a moment he heard a noise among the plants near him and saw issue from them a little man, no taller than a hearth brush. He had a book under his arm, spectacles on his crooked little nose and wore the great black cloak of a doctor.

"What are you seeking, little one?" said the Doctor; "and how is it possible that you have gained this summit?"

"Doctor, I come from the fairy Bienfaisante, to ask the plant of life to cure my poor sick mother, who is about to die."

"All those who come from the fairy Bienfaisante," said the little Doctor, raising his hat respectfully, "are most welcome. Come, my boy, I will give you the plant you seek."

The Doctor then buried himself in the botanical garden where Henry had some trouble in following him, as he was so small as to disappear entirely among the plants. At last they arrived near a bush growing by itself. The Doctor drew a little pruning-knife from his pocket, cut a bunch and gave it to Henry, saying:

"Take this and use it as the good fairy Bienfaisante directed but do not allow it to leave your hands. If you lay it down under any circumstances it will escape from you and you will never recover it."

Henry was about to thank him but the little man had disappeared in the midst of his medicinal herbs, and he found himself alone.

"What shall I do now in order to arrive quickly at home? If I encounter on my return the same obstacles which met me as I came up the mountain, I shall perhaps lose my plant, my dear plant, which should restore my dear mother to life."

Happily Henry now remembered the stick which the Wolf had given him.

"Well, let us see," said he, "if this stick has really the power to carry me home."

Saying this, he mounted the stick and wished himself at home. In the same moment he felt himself raised in the air, through which he passed with the rapidity of lightning and found himself almost instantly by his mother's bed.

Henry sprang to his mother and embraced her tenderly. But she neither saw nor heard him. He lost no time, but pressed the plant of life upon her lips. At the same moment she opened her eyes, threw her arms around Henry's neck and exclaimed:

"My child! my dear Henry! I have been very sick but now I feel almost well. I am hungry."

Then, looking at him in amazement, she said: "How you have grown, my darling! How is this? How can you have changed so in a few days?"

Henry had indeed grown a head taller. Two years, seven months and six days had passed away since he left his home. He was now nearly ten years old. Before he had time to answer, the window opened and the good fairy Bienfaisante appeared. She embraced Henry and, approaching the couch of his mother, related to her all that little Henry had done and suffered, the dangers he had dared, the fatigues he endured; the courage, the patience, the goodness he had manifested. Henry blushed on hearing himself thus praised by the fairy. His mother pressed him to her heart, and covered him with kisses. After the first moments of happiness and emotion had passed away, the fairy said:

"Now, Henry, you can make use of the present of the little Old Man and the Giant of the mountain."

Henry drew out his little box and opened it. Immediately there issued from it a crowd of little workmen, not larger than bees, who filled the room. They began to work with such promptitude that in a quarter of an hour they had built and furnished a beautiful house in the midst of a lovely garden with a thick wood on one side and a beautiful meadow on the other.

"All this is yours, my brave Henry," said the fairy. "The Giant's thistle will obtain for you all that is necessary. The Wolf's staff will transport you where you wish. The Cat's claw will preserve your health and your youth and also that of your dear mother. Adieu, Henry! Be happy and never forget that virtue and filial love are always recompensed."

Henry threw himself on his knees before the fairy who gave him her hand to kiss, smiled upon him and disappeared.

Henry's mother had a great desire to arise from her bed and admire her new house, her garden, her woods and her meadow. But, alas! she had no dress. During her first illness she had made Henry sell all that she possessed, as they were suffering for bread.

"Alas! alas! my child, I cannot leave my bed. I have neither dresses nor shoes."

"You shall have all those things, dear mother," exclaimed Henry.

Drawing his thistle from his pocket, he smelled it while he wished for dresses, linen, shoes for his mother and himself and also for linen for the house. At the same moment the presses were filled with linen, his mother was dressed in a good and beautiful robe of merino and Henry completely clothed in blue cloth, with good, substantial shoes. They both uttered a cry of joy. His mother sprang from her bed to run through the house with Henry. Nothing was wanting. Everywhere the furniture was good and comfortable. The kitchen was filled with pots and kettles; but there was nothing in them.

Henry again put his thistle to his nose and desired to have a good dinner served up.

A table soon appeared, with good smoking soup, a splendid leg of lamb, a roasted pullet and good salad. They took seats at the table with the appetite of those who had not eaten for three years. The soup was soon swallowed, the leg of lamb entirely eaten, then the pullet, then the salad.

When their hunger was thus appeased, the mother,

aided by Henry, took off the cloth, washed and arranged all the dishes and then put the kitchen in perfect order. They then made up their beds with the sheets they found in the presses and went happily to bed, thanking God and the good fairy Bienfaisante. The mother also gave grateful thanks for her dear son Henry.

They lived thus most happily, they wanted nothing—the thistle provided everything. They did not grow old or sick—the claw cured every ill. They never used the staff, as they were too happy at home ever to desire to leave it.

Henry asked of his thistle only two cows, two good horses and the necessaries of life for every day. He wished for nothing superfluous, either in clothing or food and thus he preserved his thistle as long as he lived. It is not known when they died. It is supposed that the Queen of the Fairies made them immortal and transported them to her palace, where they still are.

The Princess Rosette

HISTORY OF PRINCESS ROSETTE

THE FARM

THERE was once a king and queen, who had three daughters. The two eldest were twins—Orangine and Roussette—and their parents loved them very dearly. They were beautiful and intelligent, but they were not very good. In this they resembled the king and queen. The third princess was called Rosette and was three years younger than her sisters. She was as amiable as she was handsome, as good as she was beautiful.

The fairy Puissante was Rosette's godmother and this made her two sisters, Orangine and Roussette, very jealous. They were angry because they also had not a fairy for their godmother.

Some days after the birth of Rosette, the king and queen sent her to the country, on a farm, to be nursed. Rosette lived happily here for fifteen years without her parents coming once to see her. Every year they sent a small sum of money to the farmer to pay Rosette's expenses and asked some questions as to her health, but they never came to see her nor disturbed themselves about her education.

Rosette would indeed have been very rude and ignorant if her good godmother, the fairy Puissante, had not sent her teachers and all that was necessary. In this way Rosette learned to read, to write, to keep accounts and to work beautifully. She became an accomplished musician, she knew how to draw and spoke several languages.

Rosette was the most beautiful, the most attractive, the most amiable and the most excellent princess in the whole world. She had never disobeyed her nurse or godmother, and had therefore never been reproved. She did not regret her father and mother, as she did not know them and she did not desire any other home than the farm where she had been so happy.

One day when Rosette was seated on a bench before the door, she saw a man arrive in a laced hat and coat; he approached her and asked if he could speak to the princess Rosette.

"Yes, without doubt," answered the princess; "I am the princess Rosette.'

She saw a man arrive in a laced hat and coat

"Then, princess," said the man, respectfully taking off his hat, "be graciously pleased to receive this letter, which the king your father has charged me to deliver to you."

Rosette took the letter, opened it, and read the following:

"Rosette: Your sisters are now eighteen years old and it is time they were married. I have invited the princes and princesses of all the kingdoms of the earth to come and assist at a festival which I intend to give in order to choose husbands for Orangine and Roussette. You are now fifteen years old and can properly appear at this festival. You may come and pass three days with me. I will send for you in eight days. I cannot send you any money for your toilet as I am now at great expense for your sisters; besides, no one will look at you. Come, therefore, in any clothes you please.

"THE KING YOUR FATHER."

Rosette ran quickly to show this letter to her nurse.

"Are you pleased, Rosette, to go to this festival?"

"Yes, my good nurse, I am delighted. I will enjoy myself and become acquainted with my father, mother and my sisters and then I will return to you."

"But," said the nurse, shaking her head, "what dress will you wear, my poor child?"

"My beautiful robe of white percale which I always wear on holidays, my dear nurse."

"My poor little one, that robe is indeed very suitable for the country but would appear miserably poor at a party of kings and princes."

"Of what consequence is all this, nurse? My father himself has said that no one will look at me. This thought will make me much more at my ease. I shall see all and no one will see me."

The nurse sighed but said nothing and began immediately to mend, whiten and smooth Rosette's white robe.

The day before the king was to send for her, the nurse called her and said:

"My dear child, here is your dress for the king's festival; be very careful with it as I shall not be there to whiten and smooth it for you."

"Thanks, my good nurse; be satisfied—I will take great care."

The nurse now packed in a little trunk the percale robe and white skirt, a pair of cotton stockings and black shoes and then a little bouquet of flowers for Rosette to wear in her hair. Just as she was about to close the trunk, the window opened violently and the fairy Puissante entered.

"You are going, then, to your father's court, my dear Rosette?" said the fairy.

"Yes, dear godmother, but only for three days."

"But what dress have you prepared for those three days?"

"Look, godmother! look!" and she pointed to the trunk, which was still open.

The fairy smiled, drew a small bottle from her pocket and said: "I intend that my dear Rosette shall make a sensation by her dress. This is unworthy of her."

The fairy opened the bottle, and threw some drops of the liquid it contained upon the robe, which became a coarse India rubber cloth; then a drop upon the cotton stockings, which changed into blue yarn; a third drop upon the bouquet, which became a hen's egg; a fourth upon the shoes, and they immediately changed into coarse felt.

"In this manner," said she, with a gracious air, "do I wish my Rosette to appear. You must attire yourself in all this and, to complete your toilette, here is a necklace of nuts, a band for your hair of burrs, and bracelets of dried beans." She kissed Rosette who was completely stupefied. The fairy then disappeared and the nurse burst into tears.

"Alas! it was not worth my while to give myself all the trouble of preparing this poor robe. Oh, my poor Rosette! Do not go to this festival. Pretend you are ill, my child."

"No," said Rosette; "that would be to displease my godmother. I am sure that she does what is best for me. She is much wiser than I am. I will go and I will wear all that my godmother has brought me." And the good and obedient Rosette thought no more of her dress. She went to bed and slept tranquilly.

She had scarce arranged her hair and dressed herself in the morning when the chariot of the fairy came for her. She embraced her nurse, took her little trunk and departed.

ROSETTE AT THE COURT OF THE KING HER FATHER

THEY were but two hours on the way, for the king's capital was only ten leagues from the farm. When Rosette arrived, she was surprised to see that she had to descend in a little, dirty court-yard, where a page attended her.

"Come, princess, I am commissioned to conduct you to your chamber."

"Can I not see the queen my mother?" asked Rosette, timidly.

"In two hours, princess, when they are assembled for dinner, you will see her. In the mean time you can dress."

Rosette followed the page, who led her through a long corridor, at the end of which was a narrow staircase. She ascended, slowly, after a long, long time arriving at another corridor where she entered the chamber destined for her.

The queen had lodged Rosette in one of the servants' rooms. The little page placed Rosette's modest trunk in a corner and said, with an air of embarrassment,

"Pardon me, princess, for having led you into this chamber, so unworthy of you. The queen has disposed of all the other apartments for her guests, the kings, queens, princes and princesses. There was no other room vacant and——"

"Well, well," said Rosette, smiling, "I shall not blame you. Besides, I shall be very comfortable."

"I will come for you, princess, to lead you to the king and queen at the proper hour."

"I will be ready," said Rosette; "adieu, pretty page."

Rosette now unpacked her trunk. Her heart was beating and swelling tumultuously. Sighing heavily, she drew out her robe of coarse cloth and the other articles of her toilette. Rosette was very adroit. She arranged her exquisite blonde hair most beautifully, with a pullet's feather and a band made of burrs. Her head-dress was indeed so charming that it made her a hundred times more lovely. When she had put on her shoes and stockings and her robe, what was her amazement to see that it was made of gold brocade, embroidered with rubies of marvellous beauty; her coarse heavy shoes were now white satin, adorned with buckles of one single ruby of wonderful splendour; her stockings were of silk and as fine as a spider's web; her necklace was of rubies surrounded with large diamonds; her bracelets of diamonds, the most splendid that had ever been seen.

Rosette now ran to the glass and saw that the pullet's wing had become a magnificent locket and that the pendant was a carbuncle of such beauty and brilliancy that a fairy alone could possess it.

Rosette, happy, delighted, exultant, danced around the little room and thanked her good godmother aloud for having tested her obedience and thus magnificently rewarded it.

The page now knocked at the door, entered and started back, dazzled by the beauty of Rosette and the magnificence of her toilette. Rosette followed him. They descended the stairs, passed through many apartments and at last entered a suite of superb salons, filled with kings, queens and nobles. Every one who saw Rosette paused and turned to admire her. The modest princess, however, was ashamed to be thus gazed at and did not dare raise her eyes. At last the page paused and said to Rosette:

"Princess, behold the queen your mother and the king!"

Rosette raised her eyes and saw just before her the king and queen who regarded her with a comic surprise.

"Madam," said the king at last to her, "be graciously pleased to tell me your name. You are no doubt some great queen or still greater fairy whose unexpected presence is an honor and a happiness for us."

"Sire," said Rosette, falling gracefully upon her knees,

"I am neither a great queen nor a powerful fairy but your daughter Rosette, for whom you were kind enough to send."

"Rosette!" exclaimed the queen; "Rosette clothed more magnificently than I have ever been! Who, then, miss, has given you all these beautiful things?"

"My godmother, madam. Graciously permit me, madam, to kiss your hand and present me to my sisters."

The queen gave her hand coldly. Then pointing to Orangine and Roussette, who were by her side, she said: "There are your sisters."

Poor Rosette, saddened by this cold welcome from her father and mother, turned gladly towards her sisters and wished to embrace them but they drew back with terror, fearing that while embracing them Rosette would displace the red and white with which they were painted. Orangine covered herself with white to conceal her yellow skin and Roussette to hide her ugly freckles.

Rosette was repulsed by her sisters but was soon surrounded by the ladies of the court and all the invited princes. As she conversed with ready grace and goodness and spoke several languages she charmed all those who approached her. Orangine and Roussette were frightfully jealous. The king and queen were furious for Rosette absorbed all attention; no one paid any attention to the sisters.

At table the young prince Charmant, who was monarch of the most magnificent and beautiful of all the kingdoms of the earth and whom Orangine hoped to wed, placed himself by the side of Rosette and was completely absorbed in her during the repast.

After dinner, Orangine and Roussette, in order to draw some attention towards themselves, sang a duet. They sang indeed admirably and accompanied themselves on the harp. Rosette who was truly good and wished her sister to love her, applauded them rapturously and complimented them on their talent.

Orangine, in place of being touched by this generous sentiment and hoping to play her sister a malicious trick, now insisted upon her singing. Rosette for some time modestly refused. Her sisters, who supposed that she did not know how to sing, were insistent. The queen herself, desiring to humiliate poor Rosette, joined her entreaties to those of Orangine and Roussette and in fact commanded the young princess to sing.

Rosette curtsied to the queen. "I obey, madam," said she.

She took the harp and the enchanting grace of her position astonished her sisters. They would have been glad indeed to interrupt her when she commenced her prelude for they saw at a glance that her talent was much superior to theirs. But when, in a beautiful and melodious voice, she sang a romance, composed by herself on the happiness of being good and beloved there was an outbreak of admiration, the enthusiasm became general and her sisters almost fainted with jealousy and envy.

Charmant was transported with admiration. He approached Rosette, his eyes moistened with tears and said to her:

"Enchanting and lovely princess, I have never heard so touching a voice. Can I not have the happiness of hearing you once more?"

Rosette, who was painfully aware of the jealousy of her sisters, excused herself, saying she was fatigued. Prince Charmant, who had clear intellect and penetration, divined the true motive of her refusal and admired Rosette still more for her delicacy. The queen, irritated by the success of Rosette, terminated the party at an early hour and retired.

Rosette returned to her little room and undressed herself. She removed her robe and her ornaments and put them in a superb case of ebony which she found in her room. Much to her surprise, she found in her little trunk the robe of coarse cloth, the pullet feather, the necklace of nuts, the burrs, the dry beans, the coarse shoes of felt and the blue yarn stockings. She would not allow herself, however, to be disquieted, certain that her good godmother would come to her assistance at the proper time. Rosette was indeed saddened by the coldness of her parents and the jealousy of her sisters; but, as she scarcely knew them, this painful impression was effaced by the remembrance of the Prince Charmant, who appeared so good and who had been so flattering in his attention to her. Rosette soon slept peacefully and awoke late in the morning.

FAMILY COUNCIL

WHILE Rosette was only occupied with smiling and pleasant thoughts, the king, the queen and the princesses Orangine and Roussette were choking with rage. They had all assembled in the queen's apartment.

"This is too horrible," said the princesses. "Why did you send for this Rosette, who has such dazzling jewels and makes herself admired and sought after by all these foolish kings and princes? Was it to humiliate us, my father, that you called us to the court at this time?"

"I swear to you, my beautiful darlings," said the king, "that it was by the order of the fairy Puissante I was compelled to write for her to come. Besides, I did not know that she was so beautiful and that——"

"So beautiful!" interrupted the princesses. "Where do you find her so beautiful? She is indeed ugly and coarse.

It is her magnificent attire alone which makes her admired. Why have you not given to us your most superb jewels and your richest robes? We have the air of young slovens by the side of this proud princess."

"And where could I possibly have found jewels as magnificent as hers? I have none which would compare with them. It is her godmother, the fairy Puissante, who has lent her these jewels."

"Why, then, did you summon a fairy to be the godmother of Rosette, when you gave to us only queens for our godmothers?"

"It was not your father who called her," cried the queen. "The fairy Puissante herself, without being called, appeared to us and signified that she would be Rosette's godmother."

"It is not worth while to spend the time in disputing and quarrelling," said the king. "It is better to occupy ourselves in finding some means of getting rid of Rosette and preventing Prince Charmant from seeing her again."

"Nothing more easy than that," said the queen. "I will have her despoiled to-morrow of her rare jewels and her beautiful robes. I will order my servants to seize her and carry her back to the farm which she shall never leave again."

The queen had scarcely uttered these words, when the fairy Puissante appeared with an angry and threatening air. "If you dare to touch Rosette," said she, with a thundering voice, "if you do not keep her at the palace, if she is not present at all the parties, you shall feel the terrible effects of my anger. You unworthy king and you heartless queen, you shall be changed into toads and you, odious daughters and sisters, shall become vipers. Dare now to touch Rosette!"

Saying these words, she disappeared.

The king, the queen and princesses were horribly frightened and separated without saying a single word but their hearts were filled with rage. The princesses slept but little and were yet more furious in the morning when they saw their eyes heavy and their features convulsed by evil passions. In vain they used rouge and powder and beat their maids. They had no longer a vestige of beauty. The king and queen were as unhappy and as despairing as the princesses and indeed they saw no remedy for their grief and disappointment.

SECOND DAY OF THE FESTIVAL

IN the morning a coarse servant brought Rosette bread and milk and offered her services to dress her. Rosette, who did not wish this rude domestic to see the change in her dress, thanked her smilingly and replied that she was in the habit of arranging her hair and dressing herself. Rosette then began her toilette. When she had washed and combed her hair she wished to arrange it with the superb carbuncle she had worn the day before but she saw with surprise that the ebony case had disappeared and in its place was a small wooden trunk, upon which there lay a folded paper. She took it and read the following directions:

"Here are your things, Rosette. Dress yourself as you were dressed yesterday, in the clothing you brought from the farm."

Rosette did not hesitate an instant, certain that her godmother would come to her help at the proper time. She arranged her pullet wing in a different manner from that of the day before, put on her dress, her necklace, her shoes, her bracelets and then stood before the glass.

When she saw her own reflection in the mirror she was amazed. She was attired in the richest and most splendid riding-suit of sky-blue velvet and pearl buttons as large as walnuts; her stockings were bordered with a wreath of pearls; her head-dress was a cap of sky-blue velvet with a long plume of dazzling whiteness, which floated down to her waist and was attached by a single pearl of unparalleled beauty and splendor. The boots were also of blue velvet embroidered in gold and pearls. Her bracelets and necklace also were of pearls, so large and so pure that a single one would have paid for the king's palace.

At the moment when Rosette was about to leave her chamber to follow the page, a sweet voice whispered in her ear, "Rosette, do not mount any other horse than the one the prince Charmant will present you."

She turned and saw no one; but she felt convinced that this counsel came from her good godmother.

"Thanks, dear godmother," she said, in low tones. She felt a sweet kiss upon her cheek and smiled with happiness and gratitude.

The little page conducted her, as the day before, into the

royal salon, where her appearance produced a greater effect than before. Her fine, sweet countenance, her splendid figure, her magnificent dress, allured all eyes and captivated all hearts.

The prince Charmant, who was evidently expecting her, advanced to meet her, offered his arm and led her to the king and queen who received her with more coldness than the day before. Orangine and Roussette were bursting with spite at the sight of the splendid appearance of Rosette. They would not even say good-day to their sister.

The good, young princess was of course somewhat embarrassed by this reception but the prince Charmant, seeing her distress, approached and asked permission to be her companion during the chase in the forest.

"It will be a great pleasure to me," replied Rosette, who did not know how to dissimulate.

"It seems to me," said he, "that I am your brother, so great is the affection which I feel for you, charming princess. Permit me to remain by your side and to defend you against all enemies."

"It will be an honor and a pleasure for me to be protected by a king so worthy of the name he bears."

Prince Charmant was enchanted by this gracious reply and, notwithstanding the malice of Orangine and Roussette, who tried in every possible way to attract him to themselves, he did not leave Rosette's side for a moment.

After breakfast they descended to the court for a ride on horseback. A page advanced to Rosette, leading a splendid black horse, which could scarcely be held by the grooms, it was so wild and vicious.

"You must not ride this horse, princess," said Prince Charmant, "it will certainly kill you. Bring another horse for the princess," he said, turning to the page.

"The king and the queen gave orders that the princess should ride no other horse than this," said the page. At this the prince exclaimed:

"Dear princess, wait but for a moment; I myself will bring you a horse worthy of you but I implore you not to mount this dangerous animal."

"I will wait your return," said Rosette, with a gracious smile.

A few moments afterwards Prince Charmant appeared, leading a magnificent horse, white as snow. The saddle was of blue velvet, embroidered in pearls and the bridle was of gold and pearls. When Rosette wished to mount, the horse knelt down and rose quietly when she had placed herself in the saddle.

Prince Charmant sprang lightly upon his beautiful steed Alezan and placed himself by the side of the princess Rosette. The king, the queen and the princesses, who had seen all this, were pale with rage but they dared say nothing for fear of the fairy Puissante.

The king gave the signal to depart. Every lady had her attendant gentleman. Orangine and Roussette were obliged to content themselves with two insignificant princes who were neither so young nor so handsome as Prince Charmant. Orangine and Roussette were so sulky that even these princes declared they would never wed princesses so uninteresting.

In place of following the chase, Prince Charmant and Rosette wandered in the beautiful shady walks of the forest, talking merrily and giving accounts of their past lives.

"But," said Charmant, "if the king your father has not allowed you to reside in his palace, how is it that he has given you such beautiful jewels, worthy of a fairy?"

"It is to my good godmother that I owe them," replied Rosette. And then she told Prince Charmant how she had been educated on a farm and that she was indebted to the fairy Puissante for everything that she knew and everything she valued. The fairy had watched over her education and granted her every wish of her heart.

Charmant listened with a lively interest and a tender compassion. And now, in his turn, he told Rosette that he had been left an orphan at the age of seven years; that the fairy Puissante had presided over his education; that she had also sent him to the festivals given by the king, telling him he would find there the perfect woman he was seeking.

"In short, I believe, dear Rosette, that I have found in

you the charming and perfect creature of whom the fairy spoke. Deign, princess, to connect your life with mine and authorize me to demand your hand of your parents."

"Before answering, dear prince, I must obtain permission of my godmother but you may be sure that I shall be very happy to pass my life with you."

The morning thus passed away most agreeably for Rosette and Charmant and they returned to the palace to dress for dinner.

Rosette entered her ugly garret and saw before her a magnificent box of rosewood, wide open. She undressed and as she removed her articles of clothing they arranged themselves in the box, which then closed firmly. She arranged her hair and dressed herself with her usual neatness and then ran to the glass. She could not suppress a cry of admiration.

Her robe was of gauze and was so fine and light, and brilliant it looked as if woven of the wings of butterflies. It was studded with diamonds as brilliant as stars. The hem of this robe, the corsage and the waist were trimmed with diamond fringe which sparkled like suns. Her hair was partly covered with a net of diamonds from which a tassel of immense diamonds fell to her shoulders. Every diamond was as large as a pear and was worth a kingdom. Her necklace and bracelets were so immense and so brilliant that you could not look at them fixedly without being blinded.

The young princess thanked her godmother most tenderly and felt again upon her fair cheek the sweet kiss of the morning. She followed the page and entered the royal salon. Prince Charmant was awaiting her at the door, offered her his arm and conducted her to the apartment of the king and queen. Rosette advanced to salute them.

Charmant saw with indignation the glances of rage and revenge which the king, queen and princesses cast upon poor Rosette. He remained by her side as he had done in the morning and was witness to the admiration which she inspired and the malice and envy of her sisters.

Rosette was indeed sad to find herself the object of hatred to her father, mother and sisters. Charmant perceived her melancholy and asked the cause. She explained it to him frankly.

"When, oh! when, my dear Rosette, will you permit me to ask your hand of your father? In my kingdom every one will love you and I more than all the rest."

"To-morrow, dear prince, I will send you the reply of my godmother whom I shall question on the subject this evening."

They were now summoned to dinner. Charmant placed himself at Rosette's side and they conversed in a most agreeable manner.

After dinner the king gave orders for the ball to commence. Orangine and Roussette, who had taken lessons for ten years, danced well but without any peculiar grace. They believed that Rosette had never had any opportunity to dance and with a mocking, malicious air, they now announced to her that it was her turn.

The modest Rosette hesitated and drew back because it was repugnant to her to show herself in public and attract the general regard. But the more she declined, the more her envious sisters insisted, hoping that she would at last suffer a real humiliation.

The queen now interfered and sternly commanded Rosette to dance. Rosette rose at once to obey the queen. Charmant, seeing her embarrassment, said to her in low tones:

"I will be your partner, dear Rosette. If you do not know a single step, let me execute it for you alone."

"Thanks, dear prince. I recognize and am grateful for your courtesy. I accept you for my partner and hope that you will not have occasion to blush for your generosity."

And now Rosette and Charmant commenced. A more animated, graceful and light dance was never seen. All present gazed at them with ever increasing admiration. Rosette was so superior in dancing to Orangine and Roussette, that they could scarcely suppress their rage. They wished to throw themselves upon the young princess, choke her and tear her diamonds from her. The king and queen,

THEY WALKED SIDE BY SIDE DURING THE REST OF THE EVENING

—*Page 127*

who had been watching them and divined their intention, stopped them, and whispered in their ears:

"Remember the threats and power of the fairy Puissante! To-morrow shall be the last day."

When the dance was concluded, the most rapturous applause resounded throughout the hall and every one entreated Charmant and Rosette to repeat the dance. As they felt no fatigue they did not wish to seem disobliging and executed a new dance, more graceful and attractive than the first.

Orangine and Roussette could no longer control themselves. They were suffocating with rage, fainted and were carried from the room. They had become so marked by the passions of envy and rage that they had lost every vestige of beauty and no one had any sympathy for them, as all had seen their jealousy and wickedness.

The applause and enthusiasm for Rosette and Charmant were so overpowering that they sought refuge in the garden. They walked side by side during the rest of the evening, and talked merrily and happily over their plans for the future, if the fairy Puissante would permit them to unite the smooth current of their lives. The diamonds of Rosette sparkled with such brilliancy that the alleys where they walked and the little groves where they seated themselves, seemed illuminated by a thousand stars. At last it was necessary to separate.

"To-morrow!" said Rosette, "to-morrow I hope to say, *yours eternally.*"

Rosette entered her little room. As she undressed, her clothing arranged itself as the day before in the case. This new case was of carved ivory and studded with turquoise nails. When Rosette had lain down peacefully upon her bed she put out the light, and said, in a low voice:

"My dear, good godmother, to-morrow I must give a definite answer to Prince Charmant. Dictate my response, dear godmother. I will obey your command, no matter how painful it may be."

"Say yes, my dear Rosette, to Prince Charmant," replied the soft voice of the fairy. "I myself arranged this marriage. It was to make you acquainted with Prince Charmant that I forced your father to invite you to this festival."

Rosette thanked the kind fairy and slept the sleep of innocence, after having felt the maternal lips of her good protectress upon her cheeks.

THIRD AND LAST DAY OF THE FESTIVAL

WHILE Rosette was thus sleeping peacefully, the king, the queen, and Orangine and Roussette, purple with rage, were quarrelling and disputing amongst themselves. Each was accusing the other of having brought about the triumph of Rosette and their own humiliating defeat. One last hope remained for them. In the morning there was to be a chariot race. Each chariot was to be drawn by two horses and driven by a lady. It was resolved to give Rosette a very high chariot, drawn by two wild, untrained and prancing horses.

"Prince Charmant will have no chariot and horses to exchange," said the queen, "as he had this morning in the case of the riding-horse. It is easy to find a horse for the saddle but it will be impossible for him to find a chariot ready for the course."

The consoling thought that Rosette might be killed or

grievously wounded and disfigured on the morrow brought peace to these four wicked beings. They retired and dreamed of the next best means of ridding themselves of Rosette if the chariot race failed. Orangine and Roussette slept but little so that in the morning they were still uglier and more unprepossessing than they had appeared the day before.

Rosette, who had a tranquil conscience and contented heart, slept all night calmly. She had been much fatigued and did not wake till a late hour. Indeed, on rising she found she had scarcely time to dress. The coarse kitchen girl brought her a cup of milk and a piece of bread. This was by order of the queen who directed that she should be treated like a servant.

Rosette was not difficult to please. She ate the coarse bread and milk with appetite and began to dress. The case of carved ivory had disappeared. She put on as usual her robe of coarse cloth, her pullet's wing, and all the rude ornaments she had brought from the farm and then looked at herself in the glass.

She was attired in a riding habit of straw-colored satin, embroidered in front and at the hem with sapphires and emeralds. Her hat was of white velvet, ornamented with plumes of a thousand colors, taken from the plumage of the rarest birds and attached by a sapphire larger than an egg. On her neck was a chain of sapphires, at the end of which was a watch, the face of which was opal, the back a carved sapphire and the glass diamond. This watch was always going, was never out of order and never required to be wound up.

Rosette heard her page at the door and followed him. On entering the salon she perceived Prince Charmant, who was awaiting her with the most lively impatience. He sprang forward to receive her, offered his arm and said with eagerness:—

"Well, dear princess, what did the fairy say to you? What answer do you give me?"

"That which my heart dictated, sweet prince. I consecrate my life to you as you have dedicated yours to me."

"Thanks! a thousand times thanks, dear and bewitching Rosette. When may I demand your hand of the king your father?"

"At the close of the chariot race, dear prince."

"Permit me to add to my first petition that of being married to you this very day. I cannot bear to see you subjected to the tyranny of your family and I wish to conduct you at once to my kingdom."

Rosette hesitated. The soft voice of the fairy whispered in her ear, "Accept." The same voice whispered to Charmant, "Press the marriage, prince and speak to the king without delay. Rosette's life is in danger and during eight days from the setting of the sun this evening I cannot watch over her."

Charmant trembled and repeated the fairy's words to Rosette, who replied that it was a warning they must not neglect as it undoubtedly came from the fairy Puissante.

The princess now advanced to salute the king, the queen and her sisters but they neither looked at her nor spoke to her. She was however immediately surrounded by a crowd of kings and princes, each one of whom had himself proposed to ask her hand in marriage that evening but no one had an opportunity to speak to her as Charmant never left her side a single moment.

After the repast they went down to get into the chariots. The kings and princes were to go on horseback and the ladies to drive the chariots.

The chariot designed for Rosette by the queen was now brought forward. Charmant seized Rosette at the moment she was about to take the reins and lifted her to the ground.

"You shall not enter this chariot, princess. Look at these wild ungovernable horses."

Rosette now saw that it took four men to hold each of the horses and that they were prancing and jumping alarmingly.

At this instant a pretty little jockey, attired in a straw-colored satin vest, with blue ribbon knots, exclaimed in silvery tones:—

"The equipage of the Princess Rosette!"

And now a little chariot of pearls and mother-of-pearl, drawn by two magnificent steeds with harness of straw-colored velvet ornamented with sapphires, drew up before the princess.

Charmant scarcely knew whether to allow Rosette to mount this unknown chariot for he still feared some cunning wickedness of the king and queen. But the voice of the fairy sounded in his ear:—

"Allow Rosette to ascend the chariot; these horses are a present from me. Follow them wherever they may take Rosette. The day is advancing. I have but a few hours left in which I can be of service to Rosette and she must be safe in your kingdom before the day closes."

Charmant assisted Rosette to ascend the chariot and sprang upon his horse. A few moments afterwards, two chariots driven by veiled women advanced in front of Rosette. One of them dashed her chariot with such violence against that of Rosette, that the little chariot of mother-of-pearl would inevitably have been crushed had it not been constructed by fairies. The heavy and massive chariot was dashed to pieces instead of Rosette's. The veiled woman was thrown upon the stones, where she remained immovable whilst Rosette, who had recognized Orangine, tried to stop her own horses. The other chariot now dashed against that of Rosette and was crushed like the first and the veiled woman was also dashed upon the stones, which seemed placed there to receive her.

Rosette recognised Roussette and was about to descend from her chariot when Charmant interfered, and said: "Listen, Rosette!"

A voice whispered, "Go, flee quickly! The king is pursuing you with a great company to kill you both. The sun will set in a few hours. I have barely time to rescue you from this danger so give my horses the reins; Charmant, abandon yours."

Charmant sprang into the chariot by the side of Rosette, who was more dead than alive. The superb steeds set off with such marvellous speed that they made more than twenty leagues an hour. For a long time they knew that they were pursued by the king with a numerous troop of armed men but they could not overtake the horses of the fairy. The chariot still flew on with lightning haste; the horses increased their speed till at last they made a hundred leagues an hour. During six hours they kept up this rate and then drew up at the foot of the stairs of Prince Charmant.

The whole palace was illuminated and all the courtiers were waiting at the entrance in their most magnificent costumes to welcome the princess and the prince.

The prince and Rosette were amazed, not knowing how to understand this unexpected reception. Charmant had just assisted the princess to descend from the chariot, when they saw before them the fairy Puissante, who said:—

"Most welcome to your kingdom. Prince Charmant, follow me; all is prepared for your marriage. Conduct Rosette to her room that she may change her dress, whilst I explain to you all the events of this day which seem so incomprehensible to you. I have one hour at my disposal."

The fairy and Charmant now led Rosette to an apartment, ornamented with the most exquisite taste, where she found her maids waiting to attend upon her.

"I will return to seek you in a short time, my dear Rosette," said the fairy; "my moments are counted."

She departed with Charmant and said to him:—

"The hatred of the king and queen against Rosette had become so intense that they had blindly resolved to defy my vengeance and to get rid of Rosette. Seeing that their cunning arrangements in the chariot race had not succeeded after I substituted my horses for those which would certainly have killed Rosette, they resolved to have recourse to violence. The king employed a band of brigands, who swore to him a blind obedience; they pursued your steps with vengeance in their hearts and as the king knew your love for Rosette and foresaw that you would defend her to the death, he was resolved to sacrifice you also to his hatred. Orangine and Roussette, ignorant of this last project of the king, attempted to kill Rosette, as you have seen, by dashing their heavy chariots violently against the light chariot of the princess. I have punished them as they deserved.

"Orangine and Roussette have had their faces so crushed and wounded by the stones that they have become frightful. I have aroused them from their state of unconsciousness, cured their wounds but left the hideous scars to disfigure them. I have deprived them of all their rich clothing and dressed them like peasants and I married them at once to two brutal ostlers whom I commissioned to beat and maltreat them until their wicked hearts are changed—and this I think will never take place.

"As to the king and queen, I have changed them into beasts of burden and given them to wicked and cruel masters who will make them suffer for all their brutality to Rosette. Besides this, they have all been transported into your kingdom and they will be compelled to hear unceasingly the praises of Rosette and her husband.

"I have but one piece of advice to give you, dear prince; hide from Rosette the punishment I have inflicted upon her parents and sisters. She is so good and tender-hearted that her happiness would be affected by it, but I ought not and will not take pity upon wicked people whose hearts are so vicious and unrepentant."

Charmant thanked the fairy eagerly and promised silence. They now returned to Rosette, who was clothed in her wedding-robe, prepared by the fairy Puissante.

It was a tissue of dazzling golden gauze, embroidered

with garlands of flowers and birds, in stones of all colors, of admirable beauty; the jewels which formed the birds were so disposed as to produce, at every motion of Rosette, a warbling more melodious than the sweetest music. Upon her head was a crown of flowers made of gems still more beautiful and rare than those on her robe. Her neck and arms were covered with carbuncles more brilliant than the sun.

Charmant was completely dazzled by his bride's beauty but the fairy recalled him from his ecstasy by saying:—

"Quick! quick! onward! I have but half an hour, after which I must give myself up to the queen of the fairies and lose my power for eight days. We are all subject to this law and nothing can free us from it."

Charmant presented his hand to Rosette and the fairy preceded them. They walked towards the chapel which was brilliantly illuminated and here Charmant and Rosette received the nuptial benediction. On returning to the parlor, they perceived that the fairy had disappeared, but, as they were sure of again seeing her in eight days her absence caused them no anxiety. Charmant presented the new queen to his court. Everybody found her as charming and good as the prince and they felt disposed to love her as they loved him.

With a most amiable and thoughtful attention, the fairy had transported the farm, upon which Rosette had been so happy, and all its occupants into Charmant's kingdom.

The fairy must give herself up to the queen and lose her power for eight days

This farm was placed at the end of the park, so that Rosette could walk there every day and see her good nurse. The fairy had also brought into the palace all those cases which contained the rich dresses in which Rosette had been so triumphant at the festivals.

Rosette and Charmant were very happy and loved each other tenderly always. Rosette never knew the terrible punishment of her father, mother and sisters. When she asked Charmant the fate of her sisters, he told her that their faces were much disfigured by their fall amongst the stones but they were well and married and the good fairy expressly forbade Rosette to think of them. She spoke of them no more.

As to Orangine and Roussette, the more unhappy they were, the more cruel and wicked their hearts became, so the fairy allowed them to remain always ugly and in the most degraded ranks of life.

The king and queen, changed into beasts of burden, found their only consolation in biting and kicking everything that came within their reach. They were obliged to carry their masters to festivals given in honor of Rosette's marriage and they were mad with rage when they heard the praises lavished upon the young couple and in seeing Rosette pass by, beautiful, radiant and adored by Charmant.

The fairy had resolved that they should not return to their original forms till their hearts were changed. It is said that six thousand years have passed, and they are still beasts of burden.

The Little Grey Mouse

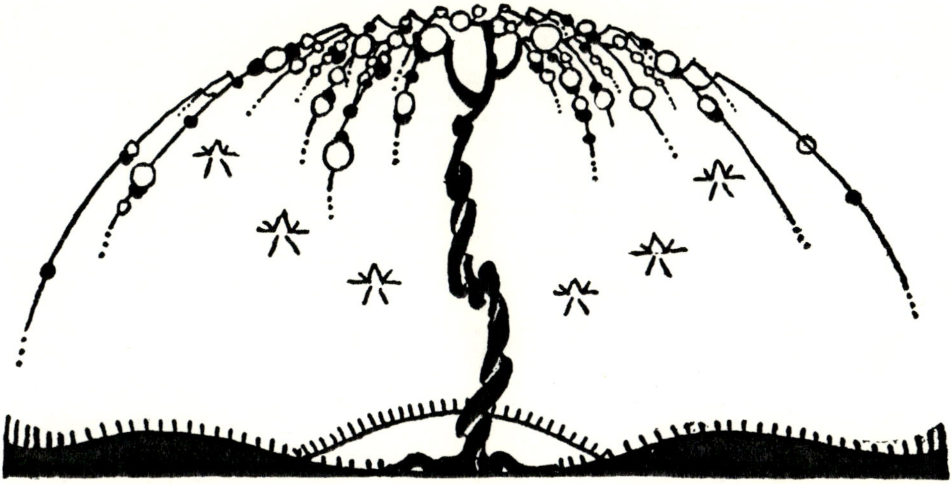

THE LITTLE GREY MOUSE

THE LITTLE HOUSE

THERE was once a man named Prudent, who was a widower and he lived alone with his little daughter. His wife had died a few days after the birth of this little girl, who was named Rosalie.

Rosalie's father had a large fortune. He lived in a great house, which belonged to him. This house was surrounded by a large garden in which Rosalie walked whenever she pleased to do so.

She had been trained with great tenderness and gentleness but her father had accustomed her to the most unquestioning obedience. He forbade her positively to ask him any useless questions or to insist upon knowing anything he did not wish to tell her. In this way, by unceasing care and

Rosalie never left the park, which was surrounded by high walls

watchfulness, he had almost succeeded in curing one of Rosalie's great faults, a fault indeed unfortunately too common—curiosity.

Rosalie never left the park, which was surrounded by high walls. She never saw any one but her father. They had no domestic in the house; everything seemed to be done of itself. She always had what she wanted—clothing, books, work, and playthings. Her father educated her himself and although she was nearly fifteen years old, she was never weary and never thought that she might live otherwise and might see more of the world.

There was a little house at the end of the park without windows and with but one door, which was always locked. Rosalie's father entered this house every day and always carried the key about his person. Rosalie thought it was only a little hut in which the garden-tools were kept. She never thought of speaking about it but one day, when she was seeking a watering-pot for her flowers, she said to him:—

"Father, please give me the key of the little house in the garden."

"What do you want with this key, Rosalie?"

"I want a watering-pot and I think I could find one in that little house."

"No, Rosalie, there is no watering-pot there."

Prudent's voice trembled so in pronouncing these words that Rosalie looked up with surprise, and saw that his face was pale and his forehead bathed in perspiration.

"What is the matter, father?" said she, alarmed.

"Nothing, daughter, nothing."

"It was my asking for the key which agitated you so violently, father. What does this little house contain which frightens you so much?"

"Rosalie, Rosalie! you do not know what you are saying. Go and look for your watering-pot in the greenhouse."

"But, father, what is there in the little garden-house?"

"Nothing that can interest you, Rosalie."

"But why do you go there every day without permitting me to go with you?"

"Rosalie, you know that I do not like to be questioned and that curiosity is the greatest defect in your character."

Rosalie said no more but she remained very thoughtful. This little house, of which she had never before thought, was now constantly in her mind.

"What can be concealed there?" she said to herself. "How pale my father turned when I asked his permission to enter! I am sure he thought I should be in some sort of danger. But why does he go there himself every day? It is no doubt to carry food to some ferocious beast confined there. But if it was some wild animal, would I not hear it roar or howl or shake the house? No, I have never heard any sound from this cabin. It cannot then be a beast. Besides, if it was a ferocious beast, it would devour my father when he entered alone. Perhaps, however, it is chained. But if it is indeed chained, then there would be no danger for me. What can it be? A prisoner? My father is good, he would not deprive any unfortunate innocent of light and liberty. Well, I absolutely must discover this mystery. How shall I manage it? If I could only secretly get the key from my father for a half hour! Perhaps some day he will forget it."

Rosalie was aroused from this chain of reflection by her father, who called to her with a strangely agitated voice.

"Here, father—I am coming."

She entered the house and looked steadily at her father. His pale, sad countenance indicated great agitation.

More than ever curious, she resolved to feign gaiety and indifference in order to allay her father's suspicions and make him feel secure. In this way she thought she might perhaps obtain possession of the key at some future time. He might not always think of it if she herself seemed to have forgotten it.

They seated themselves at the table. Prudent ate but little and was sad and silent, in spite of his efforts to appear gay. Rosalie, however, seemed so thoughtless and bright that her father at last recovered his accustomed good spirits.

Rosalie would be fifteen years old in three weeks. Her father had promised an agreeable surprise for this event. A few days passed peacefully away. There remained but fifteen days before her birth-day. One morning Prudent said to Rosalie:—

"My dear child, I am compelled to be absent for one hour. I must go out to arrange something for your birth-day. Wait for me in the house, my dear. Do not yield yourself up to idle curiosity. In fifteen days you will know all that you desire to know, for I read your thoughts and I know what occupies your mind. Adieu, my daughter, beware of curiosity!"

Prudent embraced his daughter tenderly and withdrew, leaving her with great reluctance.

As soon as he was out of sight, Rosalie ran to her father's room and what was her joy to see the key forgotten upon the table! She seized it and ran quickly to the end of the park. Arrived at the little house, she remembered the words of her father, "Beware of curiosity!" She hesitated, and was upon the point of returning the key without having looked at the house, when she thought she heard a light groan. She put her ear against the door and heard a very little voice singing softly:—

"A lonely prisoner I pine,
No hope of freedom now is mine;
I soon must draw my latest breath,
And in this dungeon meet my death."

"No doubt," said Rosalie to herself, "this is some unfortunate creature whom my father holds captive."

Tapping softly upon the door, she said: "Who are you, and what can I do for you?"

"Open the door, Rosalie! I pray you open the door!"

"But why are you a prisoner? Have you not committed some crime?"

"Alas! no, Rosalie. An enchanter keeps me here a

prisoner. Save me and I will prove my gratitude by telling you truly who I am."

Rosalie no longer hesitated: her curiosity was stronger than her obedience. She put the key in the lock, but her hand trembled so that she could not open it. She was about to give up the effort, when the little voice continued:—

"Rosalie, that which I have to tell you will teach you many things which will interest you. Your father is not what he appears to be."

At these words Rosalie made a last effort, the key turned and the door opened.

THE FAIRY DETESTABLE

ROSALIE looked in eagerly. The little house was dark; she could see nothing but she heard the little voice:—

"Thanks, Rosalie, it is to you that I owe my deliverance."

The voice seemed to come from the earth. She looked, and saw in a corner two brilliant little eyes gazing at her maliciously.

"My cunning trick has succeeded, Rosalie, and betrayed you into yielding to your curiosity. If I had not spoken and sung you would have returned with the key and I should have been lost. Now that you have set me at liberty, you and your father are both in my power."

Rosalie did not yet fully comprehend the extent of the misfortune she had brought about by her disobedience. She knew, however, that it was a dangerous foe which her father had held captive and she wished to retire and close the door.

"Stop, Rosalie! It is no longer in your power to keep me in this odious prison from which I never could have escaped if you had waited until your fifteenth birth-day."

At this moment the little house disappeared entirely, and Rosalie saw with the greatest consternation that the key alone remained in her hand. She now saw at her side a small gray mouse who gazed at her with its sparkling little eyes and began to laugh in a thin, discordant voice.

"Ha! ha! ha! What a frightened air you have, Rosalie! In truth you amuse me very much. But it is lucky for me that you had so much curiosity. It has been nearly fifteen years since I was shut up in this frightful prison, having no power to injure your father, whom I hate, or to bring any evil upon you, whom I detest because you are his daughter."

"Who are you, then, wicked mouse?"

"I am the mortal enemy of your family, my pet. I call myself the fairy Detestable and the name suits me, I assure you. All the world hates me and I hate all the world. I shall follow you now for the rest of your life, wherever you go."

"Go away at once, miserable creature! A mouse is not to be feared and I will find a way to get rid of you."

"We shall see, my pet! I shall remain at your side wherever you go!"

The broom was on fire at once, blazed up and burned her hands

Rosalie now ran rapidly towards the house; every time she turned she saw the mouse galloping after her, and laughing with a mocking air. Arrived at the house, she tried to crush the mouse in the door, but it remained open in spite of every effort she could make and the mouse remained quietly upon the door-sill.

"Wait awhile, wicked monster!" cried Rosalie, beside herself with rage and terror.

She seized a broom and tried to dash it violently against the mouse but the broom was on fire at once, blazed up and burned her hands; she threw it quickly to the floor and pushed it into the chimney with her foot, lest it should set fire to the house. Then seizing a kettle which was boiling on the fire, she emptied it upon the mouse but the boiling water was changed into good fresh milk and the mouse commenced drinking it, saying:—

"How exceedingly amiable you are, Rosalie! Not content with having released me from captivity, you give me an excellent breakfast."

Poor Rosalie now began to weep bitterly. She was utterly at a loss what to do, when she heard her father entering.

"My father!" cried she, "my father! Oh! cruel mouse, I beseech you in pity to go away that my father may not see you!"

"No, I shall not go but I will hide myself behind your heels until your father knows of your disobedience."

The mouse had scarcely concealed herself behind Rosalie, when Prudent entered. He looked at Rosalie, whose paleness and embarrassed air betrayed her fear.

"Rosalie," said Prudent, with a trembling voice, "I forgot the key of the little garden-house; have you found it?"

"Here it is, father," said Rosalie, presenting it to him, and coloring deeply.

"How did this cream come to be upset on the floor?"

"Father, it was the cat."

"The cat? Impossible. The cat brought a vessel of milk to the middle of the room and upset it there?"

"No! no! father, it was I that did it; in carrying it, I accidentally overturned it."

Rosalie spoke in a low voice, and dared not look at her father.

"Take the broom, Rosalie, and sweep up this cream."

"There is no broom, father."

"No broom! there was one when I left the house."

"I burned it, father, accidentally, by ——— by ———"

She paused—her father looked fixedly at her, threw a searching unquiet glance about the room, sighed and turned his steps slowly towards the little house in the garden.

Rosalie fell sobbing bitterly upon a chair; the mouse did not stir. A few moments afterwards, Prudent entered hastily, his countenance marked with horror.

"Rosalie! unhappy child! what have you done? You have yielded to your fatal curiosity and released our most cruel enemy from prison."

"Pardon me, father! oh pardon me!" she cried, throwing herself at his feet; "I was ignorant of the evil I did."

"Misfortune is always the result of disobedience, Rosalie; disobedient children think they are only committing a small fault, when they are doing the greatest injury to themselves and others."

"But, father, who and what then is this mouse, who causes you this terrible fear? How, if it had so much power, could you keep it so long a prisoner and why can you not put it in prison again?"

"This mouse, my unhappy child, is a wicked fairy, but very powerful. For myself, I am the genius Prudent and since you have given liberty to my enemy, I can now reveal to you that which I should have concealed until you were fifteen years old.

"I am, then, as I said to you, the genius Prudent; your dear mother was a simple mortal but her virtues and her graces touched the queen of the fairies and also the king of the genii and they permitted me to wed her. I gave a splendid festival on my marriage-day. Unfortunately I forgot to invoke the fairy Detestable, who was already irritated against me for having married a princess, after having refused one of her daughters. She was so exasperated against me that she swore an implacable hatred against me, my wife and my children. I was not terrified at her threats, as I myself had a power almost equal to her own and I was much beloved by the queen of the fairies. Many times by the power of my enchantments, I triumphed over the malicious hatred of the fairy Detestable.

"A few hours after your birth your mother was thrown

into the most violent convulsions which I could not calm. I left her for a few moments to invoke the aid of the queen of the fairies. When I returned your mother was dead.

"The wicked fairy Detestable had profited by my absence and caused her death. She was about to endow you with all the passions and vices of this evil world, when my unexpected return happily paralyzed her efforts. I interrupted her at the moment when she had endowed you with a curiosity sufficient to make you wretched and to subject you entirely to her power at fifteen years of age. By my power, united to that of the queen of the fairies, I counter-balanced this fatal influence and we decided that you should not fall under her power at fifteen years of age, unless you yielded three times under the gravest circumstances to your idle curiosity.

"At the same time the queen of the fairies, to punish the fairy Detestable, changed her into a mouse, shut her up in the little garden house, and declared that she should never leave it unless you voluntarily opened the door. Also, that she should never resume her original form of fairy unless you yielded three times to your criminal curiosity before you were fifteen years of age. Lastly, that if you resisted once the fatal passion you should be for ever released, as well as myself, from the power of the fairy Detestable.

"With great difficulty I obtained all these favors and only by promising that I would share your fate and become, like yourself, the slave of the fairy Detestable, if you weakly allowed yourself to yield three times to your curiosity. I promised solemnly to educate you in such a manner as to destroy this terrible passion, calculated to cause so many sorrows.

"For all these reasons I have confined myself and you, Rosalie, in this enclosure. I have permitted you to see no one, not even a domestic. I procured by my power all that your heart desired and I have been feeling quite satisfied in having succeeded so well with you. In three weeks you would have been fifteen, and for ever delivered from the odious yoke of the fairy Detestable.

"I was alarmed when you asked for the key of the little house, of which you had never before seemed to think. I could not conceal the painful impression which this demand made upon me. My agitation excited your curiosity. In spite of your gaiety and assumed thoughtlessness, I penetrated your thoughts, and you may judge of my grief when the queen of the fairies ordered me to make the temptation possible and the resistance meritorious by leaving the key at least once in your reach. I was thus compelled to leave it, that fatal key, and thus facilitate by my absence my own and your destruction.

"Imagine, Rosalie, what I suffered during the hour of my absence, leaving you alone with this temptation before your eyes and when I saw your embarrassment and blushes on my return, indicating to me too well that you had allowed your curiosity to master you.

"I was commanded to conceal everything from you; to tell you nothing of your birth or of the dangers which surround you, until your fifteenth birthday. If I had disobeyed, you would at once have fallen into the power of the fairy Detestable.

"And yet, Rosalie, all is not lost. You can yet repair your fault by resisting for fifteen days this terrible passion. At fifteen years of age you were to have been united to a charming prince, who is related to us, the prince Gracious. This union is yet possible.

"Ah, Rosalie! my still dear child, take pity on yourself, if you have no mercy for me and resist your curiosity."

Rosalie was on her knees before her father, her face concealed in her hands and weeping bitterly. At these words she took courage, embraced him tenderly and said to him:—

"Oh, father! I promise you solemnly that I will atone for this fault. Do not leave me, dear father! With you by me, I shall be inspired with a courage which would otherwise fail me. I dare not be deprived of your wise paternal counsel."

"Alas! Rosalie! it is no longer in my power to remain with you for I am now under the dominion of my enemy. Most certainly she will not allow me to stay by your side and warn you against the snares and temptations which she will spread at your feet. I am astonished at not having seen my cruel foe before this time. The view of my affliction and despair would have for her hard heart an irresistible charm."

"I have been near you all the time, at your daughter's feet," said the little gray mouse, in a sharp voice, stepping out and showing herself to the unfortunate genius. "I have been highly entertained at the recital of all that I have already made you suffer, and the pleasure I felt in hearing you give this account to your daughter induced me to conceal myself till this moment. Now say adieu to your dear but curious Rosalie; she must accompany me, and I forbid you to follow her."

Saying these words, she seized the hem of Rosalie's dress with her sharp little teeth and tried to draw her away. Rosalie uttered a piercing cry and clung convulsively to her father but an irresistible force bore her off. The unfortunate genius seized a stick and raised it to strike the mouse but before he had time to inflict the blow the mouse placed one of her little paws on the genius's foot and he remained as immovable as a statue. Rosalie embraced her father's knees and implored the mouse to take pity upon her but the little wretch gave one of her sharp, diabolical laughs and said:—

"Come, come, my pretty! Pity it is not here that you will find the temptations to yield twice to your irresistible fault! We will travel all over the world together and I will show you many countries in fifteen days."

The mouse pulled Rosalie without ceasing. Her arms were still clasped around her father, striving to resist the overpowering force of her enemy. The mouse uttered a discordant little cry and suddenly the house was in flames. Rosalie had sufficient presence of mind to reflect that if she allowed herself to be burned there would be no means left of saving her father, who must then remain eternally under the power of Detestable. Whereas, if she preserved her own life there remained always some chance of rescuing him.

"Adieu, adieu, dear father!" she cried; "we will meet again in fifteen days. After having given you over to your enemy, your Rosalie will yet save you."

She then tore herself away, in order not to be devoured by the flames. She ran on rapidly for some time without knowing where she was going. She walked several hours but at last, exhausted with fatigue and half dead with hunger, she resolved to approach a kind-looking woman who was seated at her door.

"Madam," said she, "will you give me a place to sleep? I am dying with hunger and fatigue. Will you not be so kind as to allow me to enter and pass the night with you?"

"How is it that so beautiful a girl as yourself is found upon the highways and what ugly animal is that with the expression of a demon which accompanies you."

Rosalie turned round and saw the little gray mouse smiling upon her mockingly. She tried to chase it away but the mouse obstinately refused to move. The good woman, seeing this contest, shook her head and said:—

"Go on your ways, my pretty one. The Evil One and his followers cannot lodge with me."

Weeping bitterly, Rosalie continued her journey, and wherever she presented herself they refused to receive her and the mouse, who never quitted her side. She entered a forest where happily she found a brook at which she quenched her thirst. She found also fruits and nuts in abundance. She drank, ate and seated herself near a tree, thinking with agony of her father and wondering what would become of him during the fifteen days.

While Rosalie was thus musing she kept her eyes closed so as not to see the wicked little gray mouse. Her fatigue, and the silence and darkness around her, brought on sleep and she slept a long time profoundly.

THE PRINCE GRACIOUS

WHILE Rosalie was thus quietly sleeping, the prince Gracious was engaged in a hunt through the forest by torch-light. The fawn, pursued fiercely by the dogs, came trembling with terror to crouch down near the brook by which Rosalie was sleeping. The dogs and gamekeepers sprang forward after the fawn. Suddenly the dogs ceased barking and grouped themselves silently around Rosalie. The prince dismounted from his horse to set the dogs again upon the trail of the deer but what was his surprise to see a lovely young girl asleep in this lonely forest! He looked carefully around but saw no one else. She was indeed alone—abandoned. On examining her more closely, he saw traces of tears upon her cheeks and indeed they were still escaping slowly from her closed eye-lids.

Rosalie was simply clothed but the richness of her silk

dress denoted wealth. Her fine white hands, her rosy nails, her beautiful chestnut locks, carefully and tastefully arranged with a gold comb, her elegant boots and necklace of pure pearls indicated elevated rank.

Rosalie did not awake, notwithstanding the stamping of the horses, the baying of the dogs and the noisy tumult made by a crowd of sportsmen.

The prince was stupefied and stood gazing steadily at Rosalie. No one present recognized her. Anxious and disquieted by this profound sleep, Prince Gracious took her hand softly. Rosalie still slept. The prince pressed her hand lightly in his but even this did not awaken her.

Turning to his officers, he said: "I cannot thus abandon this unfortunate child, who has perhaps been led astray by some design, the victim of some cruel wickedness."

"But how can she be removed while she is asleep, prince," said Hubert, his principal gamekeeper, "can we not make a litter of branches and thus remove her to some hostel in the neighborhood while your highness continues the chase?"

"Your idea is good, Hubert. Make the litter and we will immediately place her upon it, only you will not carry her to a hostel, but to my palace. This young maiden is assuredly of high birth, and she is beautiful as an angel. I will watch over her myself, so that she may receive the care and attention to which she is entitled."

Hubert, with the assistance of his men, soon arranged the litter upon which Prince Gracious spread his mantle; then approaching Rosalie, who was still sleeping softly, he raised her gently in his arms and laid her upon the cloak. At this moment Rosalie seemed to be dreaming. She smiled and murmured, in low tones:—

"My father! my father! saved for ever! The Queen of the Fairies! The Prince Gracious! I see him; he is charming!"

The prince, surprised to hear his name pronounced, did not doubt that Rosalie was a princess under some cruel enchantment. He commanded his gamekeepers to walk very softly so as not to wake her and he walked by the side of the litter.

On arriving at the palace, Prince Gracious ordered that the queen's apartment should be prepared for Rosalie. He suffered no one to touch her but carried her himself to her chamber and laid her gently upon the bed, ordering the women who were to wait upon and watch over her to apprise him as soon as she awaked. Then, casting a farewell look upon the sad, sweet face of the sleeper, he strode from the room.

Rosalie slept tranquilly until morning. The sun was shining brightly when she awoke. She looked about her with great surprise. The wicked mouse was not near her to terrify her—it had happily disappeared.

“Am I delivered from this wicked fairy Detestable?” said she, joyfully. “Am I in the hands of a fairy more powerful than herself?”

Rosalie now stepped to the window and saw many armed men and many officers, dressed in brilliant uniforms. More and more surprised, she was about to call one of the men, whom she believed to be either genii or enchanters, when she heard footsteps approaching. She turned and saw the prince Gracious, clothed in an elegant and rich hunting-dress, standing before her and regarding her with admiration. Rosalie immediately recognized the prince of her dream and cried out involuntarily:—

“The prince Gracious!”

“You know me then?” said the prince, in amazement. “How, if you have ever known me, could I have forgotten your name and features?”

“I have only seen you in my dreams, prince,” said Rosalie, blushing. “As to my name, you could not possibly know it, since I myself did not know my father’s name until yesterday.”

“And what is the name, may I ask, which has been concealed from you so long?”

Rosalie then told him all that she had heard from her father. She frankly confessed her culpable curiosity and its terrible consequences.

“Judge of my grief, prince, when I was compelled to

leave my father in order to escape from the flames which the wicked fairy had lighted; when, rejected everywhere because of the wicked mouse, I found myself exposed to death from hunger and thirst! Soon, however, a heavy sleep took possession of me, during which I had many strange dreams. I do not know how I came here or whether it is in your palace that I find myself."

Gracious then related to Rosalie how he had found her asleep in the forest and the words which he had heard her utter in her dream. He then added:—

"There is one thing your father did not tell you, Rosalie; that is, that the queen of the fairies, who is our relation, had decided that we should be married when you were fifteen years of age. It was no doubt the queen of the fairies who inspired me with the desire to go hunting by torchlight, in order that I might find you in the forest where you had wandered. Since you will be fifteen in a few days, Rosalie, deign to consider my palace as your own and command here in advance, as my queen. Your father will soon be restored to you and we will celebrate our happy marriage."

Rosalie thanked her young and handsome cousin heartily and then returned to her chamber, where she found her maids awaiting her with a wonderful selection of rich and splendid robes and head-dresses. Rosalie, who had never given much attention to her toilet, took the first dress that was presented to her. It was of rose-colored gauze, ornamented with fine lace with a head-dress of lace and moss rosebuds. Her beautiful chestnut hair was arranged in bands, forming a crown. When her toilet was completed, the prince came to conduct her to breakfast.

Rosalie ate like a person who had not dined the day before. After the repast, the prince led her to the garden and conducted her to the green-houses, which were very magnificent. At the end of one of the hot-houses there was a little rotunda, ornamented with choice flowers; in the centre of this rotunda there was a large case which seemed to contain a tree but a thick heavy cloth was thrown over it and tightly sewed together. Through the cloth however could be seen a number of points of extraordinary brilliancy.

THE TREE IN THE ROTUNDA

ROSALIE admired all the flowers very much but she waited with some impatience for the prince to remove the cloth which enveloped this mysterious tree. He left the green-house, however, without having spoken of it.

"What then, my prince, is this tree which is so carefully concealed?"

"It is the wedding present which I destine for you but you cannot see it until your fifteenth birthday," said the prince, gayly.

"But what is it that shines so brilliantly under the cloth?" said she, importunately.

"You will know all in a few days, Rosalie, and I flatter myself that you will not find my present a common affair."

"And can I not see it before my birthday?"

"No, Rosalie; the queen of the fairies has forbidden me, under heavy penalties, to show it to you until after you become my wife. I do hope that you love me enough to control your curiosity till that time."

These last words made Rosalie tremble, for they recalled to her the little gray mouse and the misfortunes which menaced her as well as her father, if she allowed herself to fall under the temptation, which, without doubt, her enemy the fairy Detestable had placed before her. She spoke no more of the mysterious case, and continued her walk with the prince. The day passed most agreeably. The prince presented her to the ladies of his court and commanded them to honor and respect in her the princess Rosalie, whom the queen of the fairies had selected as his bride. Rosalie was very amiable to every one and they all rejoiced in the idea of having so charming and lovely a queen.

The following days were passed in every species of festivity. The prince and Rosalie both saw with joyous hearts the approach of the birth-day which was to be also that of their marriage:—the prince, because he tenderly loved his cousin, and Rosalie because she loved the prince, because she desired strongly to see her father again, and also because she hoped to see what the case in the rotunda contained. She thought of this incessantly. She dreamed of it during the night and whenever she was alone she could with difficulty restrain herself from rushing to the green-house to try to discover the secret.

Finally, the last day of anticipation and anxiety arrived. In the morning Rosalie would be fifteen. The prince was much occupied with the preparations for his marriage; it was to be a very grand affair. All the good fairies of his acquaintance were to be present as well as the queen of the fairies. Rosalie found herself alone in the morning and she resolved to take a walk. While musing upon the happiness of the morrow, she involuntarily approached the green-house. She entered, smiling pensively, and found herself face to face with the cloth which covered the treasure.

"To-morrow," said she, "I shall at last know what this thick cloth conceals from me. If I wished, indeed I might see it to-day, for I plainly perceive some little openings in which I might insert my fingers and by enlarging just a little ——. In fact, who would ever know it? I would sew the cloth after having taken a glimpse. Since to-morrow is so near, when I am to see all, I may as well take a glance to-day."

Rosalie looked about her and saw no one; and, in her extreme desire to gratify her curiosity, she forgot the goodness of the prince and the dangers which menaced them all if she yielded to this temptation.

She passed her fingers through the little apertures and strained them lightly. The cloth was rent from the top to the bottom with a noise like thunder and Rosalie saw before her eyes a tree of marvellous beauty, with a coral trunk and leaves of emeralds. The seeming fruits which covered the tree were of precious stones of all colors—diamonds, sapphires, pearls, rubies, opals, topazes, all as large as the fruits they were intended to represent and of such brilliancy that Rosalie was completely dazzled by them. But scarcely had she seen this rare and unparalleled tree, when a noise louder than the first drew her from her ecstasy. She felt herself lifted up and transported to a vast plain, from which she saw the palace of the king falling in ruins and heard the most frightful cries of terror and suffering issue from its walls. Soon Rosalie saw the prince himself creep from the ruins bleeding and his clothing almost torn from him. He advanced towards her and said sadly: —

"Rosalie! ungrateful Rosalie! see what you have done to me, not only to me, but to my whole court. After what you have done, I do not doubt that you will yield a third time to your curiosity; that you will complete my misfortunes, those of your unhappy father and your own. Adieu, Rosalie, adieu! May sincere repentance atone for your ingratitude towards an unhappy prince who loved you and only sought to make you happy!"

Saying these words, he withdrew slowly.

Rosalie threw herself upon her knees, bathed in tears and called him tenderly but he disappeared without ever turning to contemplate her despair. Rosalie was about to faint away, when she heard the little discordant laugh of the gray mouse and saw it before her.

"Your thanks are due to me, my dear Rosalie, for having assisted you so well. It was I who sent you those bewitching dreams of the mysterious tree during the night. It was I who nibbled the cloth, to help you in your wish to look in. Without this last artifice of mine, I believe I should have lost you, as well as your father and your prince Gracious. One more slip, my pet, and you will be my slave for ever!"

The cruel mouse, in her malicious joy, began to dance around Rosalie; her words, wicked as they were, did not excite the anger of the guilty girl.

"This is all my fault," said she; "had it not been for my fatal curiosity and my base ingratitude, the gray mouse would not have succeeded in making me yield so readily to temptation. I must atone for all this by my sorrow, by my patience and by the firmness with which I will resist the third proof to which I am subjected, no matter how difficult it may be. Besides, I have but a few hours to wait and my dear prince has told me that his happiness and that of my dearly loved father and my own, depends upon myself."

Before her lay the smouldering ruins of the palace of the Prince Gracious. So complete had been its destruction that a cloud of dust and smoke hung over it, and hardly one stone remained upon another. The cries of those in pain were borne to her ears and added to her bitterness of feeling.

Rosalie continued to lie prone on the ground. The gray mouse employed every possible means to induce her to move from the spot. Rosalie, the poor, unhappy and guilty Rosalie, persisted in remaining in view of the ruin she had caused.

THE CASKET

THUS passed the entire day. Rosalie suffered cruelly with thirst.

"Ought I not suffer even more than I do?" she said to herself, "in order to punish me for all I have made my father and my cousin endure? I will await in this terrible spot the dawning of my fifteenth birthday."

The night was falling when an old woman who was passing by, approached and said:—

"My beautiful child, will you oblige me by taking care of this casket, which is very heavy to carry, while I go a short distance to see one of my relations?"

"Willingly, madam," replied Rosalie, who was very obliging. The old woman placed the casket in her hands, saying:—

"Many thanks, my beautiful child! I shall not be absent long. But I entreat you not to look in this casket, for it contains things—things such as you have never seen—and as you will never have an opportunity to see again. Do not handle it rudely, for it is of very fragile ware and would be very easily broken and then you would see what it contains and no one ought to see what is there concealed."

The old woman went off after saying this. Rosalie placed the casket near her and reflected on all the events which had just passed. It was now night and the old woman did not return. Rosalie now threw her eyes on the casket and saw with surprise that it illuminated the ground all around her.

"What can there be in this casket which is so brilliant?" said she.

She turned it round and round and regarded it from every side but nothing could explain this extraordinary light and she placed it carefully upon the ground, saying:—

"Of what importance is it to me what this casket contains? It is not mine but belongs to the old woman who confided it to me. I will not think of it again for fear I may be tempted to open it."

In fact, she no longer looked at it and endeavored not to think of it; she now closed her eyes, resolved to wait patiently till the dawn.

"In the morning I shall be fifteen years of age. I shall

see my father and Gracious and will have nothing more to fear from the wicked fairy."

"Rosalie! Rosalie!" said suddenly the small voice of the little mouse, "I am near you once more. I am no longer your enemy and to prove that I am not, if you wish it, I will show you what this casket contains."

Rosalie did not reply.

"Rosalie, do you not hear what I propose? I am your friend, believe me."

No reply.

Then the little gray mouse, having no time to lose, sprang upon the casket and began to gnaw the lid.

"Monster!" cried Rosalie, seizing the casket and pressing it against her bosom, "if you touch this casket again I will wring your neck."

The mouse cast a diabolical glance upon Rosalie but it dared not brave her anger. While it was meditating some other means of exciting the curiosity of Rosalie, a clock struck twelve. At the same moment the mouse uttered a cry of rage and disappointment and said to Rosalie:—

"Rosalie, the hour of your birth has just sounded. You are now fifteen; you have nothing more to fear from me. You are now beyond my power and my temptations as are also your odious father and hated prince. As to myself, I am compelled to keep this ignoble form of a mouse until I can tempt some young girl beautiful and well born as yourself to fall into my snares. Adieu, Rosalie! you can now open the casket."

Saying these words, the mouse disappeared.

Rosalie, wisely distrusting these words of her enemy, would not follow her last counsel, and resolved to guard the casket carefully till the dawn. Scarcely had she taken this resolution, when an owl, which was flying above her head, let a stone fall upon the casket, which broke into a thousand pieces. Rosalie uttered a cry of terror and at the same moment she saw before her the queen of the fairies, who said:—

"Come Rosalie, you have finally triumphed over the cruel enemy of your family. I will now restore you to your father but first you must eat and drink, as you are much exhausted."

The fairy now presented her with a rare fruit, of which a single mouthful satisfied both hunger and thirst. Then a splendid chariot, drawn by two dragons, drew up before the fairy. She entered and commanded Rosalie to do the same. Rosalie, as soon as she recovered from her surprise, thanked the queen of the fairies with all her heart for her protection and asked if she was not to see her father and the prince Gracious.

"Your father awaits you in the palace of the prince."

"But, madam, I thought that the palace of the prince was destroyed and he himself wounded sadly?"

"That, Rosalie, was only an illusion to fill you with horror and remorse at the result of your curiosity and to prevent you from falling before the third temptation. You will soon see the palace of the prince just as it was before you tore the cloth which covered the precious tree he destined for you."

As the fairy said this the chariot drew up before the palace steps. Rosalie's father and the prince were awaiting her with all the court. Rosalie first threw herself in her father's arms, then in those of the prince, who seemed to have no remembrance of the fault she had committed the day before. All was ready for the marriage ceremony which was to be celebrated immediately. All the good fairies assisted at this festival which lasted several days.

Rosalie's father lived with his child and she was completely cured of her curiosity. She was tenderly loved by Prince Gracious whom she loved fondly all her life. They had beautiful children, for whom they chose powerful fairies as godmothers in order that they might be protected against the wicked fairies and genii.

Ourson

OURSON

THE LARK AND THE TOAD

THERE was once a pretty woman named Agnella, who cultivated a farm. She lived alone with a young servant named Passerose. The farm was small but beautiful and in fine order. She had a most charming cow, which gave a quantity of milk, a cat to destroy the mice and an ass to carry her fruit, butter, vegetables, eggs, and cheese to markets every Wednesday.

No one knew up to that time how Agnella and Passerose had arrived at this unknown farm which received in the county the name of the Woodland Farm.

One evening Passerose was busy milking the pretty white cow while Agnella prepared the supper. At the moment she was placing some good soup and a plate of cream upon the table, she saw an enormous toad devouring with avidity some cherries which had been put on the ground in a vine-leaf.

"Ugly toad!" exclaimed Agnella, "I will teach you how to eat my cherries!" At the same moment she lifted the leaves which contained the cherries, and gave the toad a kick which dashed it off about ten steps. She was about to throw it from the door, when the toad uttered a sharp whistle and raised itself upon its hind legs; its great eyes were flashing, and its enormous mouth opening and shutting with rage, its whole ugly body was trembling and from its quivering throat was heard a terrible bellowing.

Agnella paused in amazement; she recoiled, indeed, to avoid the venom of the monstrous and enraged toad. She looked around for a broom to eject this hideous monster, when the toad advanced towards her, made with its fore paws a gesture of authority, and said in a voice trembling with rage:—

"You have dared to touch me with your foot! You have prevented me from satisfying my appetite with the cherries which you had placed within my reach! You have tried to expel me from your house! My vengeance shall reach you and will fall upon that which you hold most dear! You shall know and feel that the fairy Furious is not to be insulted with impunity. You shall have a son covered with coarse hair like a bear's cub and ———"

"Stop, sister," interrupted a small voice, sweet and flute-like, which seemed to come from above. Agnella raised her head and saw a lark perched on the top of the front door. "You revenge yourself too cruelly for an injury inflicted, not upon you in your character of a fairy but upon the ugly and disgusting form in which it has pleased you to disguise yourself. By my power, which is superior to yours, I forbid you to exaggerate the evil which you have already done in your blind rage and which, alas! it is not in my power to undo. And you, poor mother," she continued, turning to Agnella, "do not utterly despair; there is a possible remedy for the deformity of your child. I will accord to him the power of changing his skin with any one whom he may, by his goodness and service rendered, inspire with sufficient gratitude and affection to consent to the change. He will then resume the handsome form which would have been his if my sister, the fairy Furious, had not given you this terrible proof of her malice and cruelty."

"Alas! madam Lark," replied Agnella, "all this goodness cannot prevent my poor, unhappy son from being disgusting and like a wild beast. His very playmates will shun him as a monster."

"That is true," replied the fairy Drolette; "and the more so as it is forbidden to yourself or to Passerose to change skins with him. But I will neither abandon you nor your son. You will name him Ourson until the day when he can assume a name worthy of his birth and beauty. He must then be called the prince Marvellous."

Saying these words, the fairy flew lightly through the air and disappeared from sight.

The fairy Furious withdrew, filled with rage, walking slowly and turning every instant to gaze at Agnella with a menacing air. As she moved slowly along, she spat her venom from side to side and the grass, the plants and the bushes perished along her course. This was a venom so subtle that nothing could ever flourish on the spot again and the path is called to this day the Road of the Fairy Furious.

When Agnella found herself alone, she began to sob. Passerose, who had finished her work and saw the hour of supper approaching, entered the dining-room and with great surprise saw her mistress in tears.

"Dear queen, what is the matter? Who can have caused you this great grief? I have seen no one enter the house."

"No one has entered, my dear, except those who enter everywhere. A wicked fairy under the form of a toad and a good fairy under the appearance of a lark."

"And what have these fairies said to you, my queen, to make you weep so piteously? Has not the good fairy interfered to prevent the misfortunes which the wicked fairy wished to bring about?"

"No, my dear friend. She has somewhat lightened

Agnella and Passerose were dashed from cloud to cloud

them but it was not in her power to set them aside altogether."

Agnella then recounted all that had taken place and that she would have a son with a skin like a bear. At this narrative Passerose wept as bitterly as her mistress.

"What a misfortune!" she exclaimed. "What degradation and shame, that the heir of a great kingdom should be a bear! What will King Ferocious, your husband, say if he should ever discover us?"

"And how will he ever find us, Passerose? You know that after our flight we were swept away by a whirlwind and dashed from cloud to cloud for twelve hours with such astonishing rapidity that we found ourselves more than three thousand leagues from the kingdom of Ferocious. Besides, you know his wickedness. You know how bitterly he hates me since I prevented him from killing his brother Indolent and his sister Nonchalante. You know that I fled because he wished to kill me also. I have no reason to fear that he will pursue me for I am sure that he will wish never to see me again."

Passerose, after having wept and sobbed some time with the queen Aimee, for that was her true name, now entreated her mistress to be seated at the table.

"If we wept all night, dear queen, we could not prevent your son from being shaggy but we will endeavor to educate him so well, to make him so good, that he will not be a long time in finding some good and grateful soul who will exchange a white skin for this hairy one which the evil fairy Furious has put upon him. A beautiful present indeed! She would have done well to reserve it for herself."

The poor queen, whom we will continue to call Agnella for fear of giving information to King Ferocious, rose slowly, dried her eyes and succeeded in somewhat overcoming her sadness. Little by little the gay and cheering conversation of Passerose dissipated her forebodings. Before the close of the evening, Passerose had convinced her that Ourson would not remain a long time a bear; that he would soon resume a form worthy of a noble prince. That she would herself indeed be most happy to exchange with him, if the fairy would permit it.

Agnella and Passerose now retired to their chambers and slept peacefully.

BIRTH AND INFANCY OF OURSON

THREE months after the appearance of the toad and the cruel sentence of the fairy Furious, Agnella gave birth to a boy whom she named Ourson, as the fairy Drolette had commanded. Neither Agnella nor Passerose could decide if he was ugly or handsome for he was so hairy, so covered with long brown bristles, you could see nothing but his eyes and his mouth, and not even these unless he opened them.

If Agnella had not been his mother and if Passerose had not loved her like a sister, poor Ourson would have died from neglect for he was so frightful no one would have dared to touch him—he would have been taken for a little cub and killed with pitchforks. But Agnella was his mother and her first movement was to embrace him lovingly and, bathed in tears, to exclaim:—

"Poor little Ourson! who can ever love you well enough

to deliver you from this horrible curse? Alas! why will not the fairy permit me to make this exchange, which is allowed to another who may love you? No one can ever love you as I do."

Ourson did not reply to these endearments; he slept peacefully.

Passerose wept also in sympathy with Agnella but she was not in the habit of afflicting herself for a long time on any occasion so she dried her eyes and said to Agnella:—

"Dear queen, I am very certain that your dear son will be clothed but a short time with this villainous bear-skin and from this day I shall call him Prince Marvellous."

"I beseech you not to do so," said the queen, anxiously; "you know that the fairies love to be obeyed."

Passerose took the child, clothed it in the linen that had been prepared for it and leaned over to embrace it but she pricked her lips against the rough bristles of Ourson and drew back precipitately.

"It will not be I who will embrace you frequently, my boy," said she, in a low voice; "you prick like a real hedge-hog."

It was Passerose, however, to whom Agnella gave the charge of the little Ourson. He had nothing of the bear but his skin: he was the sweetest-tempered, the most knowing, the most affectionate child that ever was seen. Passerose soon loved him with all her heart.

As Ourson grew up he was sometimes permitted to leave the farm. He was in no danger for no one knew him in the country. The children always ran away at his approach and the women repulsed him. Men avoided him—they looked upon him as something accursed. Sometimes when Agnella went to market she put him on her donkey and took him with her and on those days she found more difficulty in selling her vegetables and cheese. The mothers fled from her, fearing that Ourson would come too near them.

Agnella wept often and vainly implored the fairy Drolette. Whenever a lark flew near her, hope was born in her breast. But the larks, alas, were real larks, fit only to make pies and not fairies in disguise.

VIOLETTE

OURSON at eight years of age was tall and strong, with magnificent eyes and a sweet voice; his bristles were no longer stiff but his hair was soft as silk and those who loved him could embrace him without being scratched, as Passerose had been the day of his birth. Ourson loved his mother tenderly and Passerose almost as well but he was often alone and very sad. He saw too well the horror he inspired and he saw also that he was unlike other children.

One day he was walking along a beautiful road which bordered on the farm. He had walked a long time and overcome with heat and fatigue he looked about him for some fresh and quiet spot for repose when he thought he saw a little object, fair and rosy, a few steps from him. Drawing near with precaution he saw a little girl asleep. She seemed to be about three years old and she was beautiful as the Loves and Graces. Her blonde hair partly covered her fair and dimpled shoulders while her soft cheeks were round and fresh and dimpled and a half smile played upon her rosy and parted lips, through which small teeth, white and even as pearls, could be seen. Her charming head was reposing upon a lovely rounded arm and the little hand was beautifully formed and white as snow. The attitude of this little girl was so graceful, so enchanting, that Ourson stood before her immovable with admiration. He watched with as much surprise as pleasure, this child sleeping as soundly and peacefully in the wood as if she had been at home in her own little bed. Ourson looked at her a long time and examined her toilet which was more rich and elegant than anything he had ever seen. Her dress was of white silk embroidered in gold; her boots were of blue satin also embroidered in gold; her stockings were silk and fine as a spider's web; magnificent bracelets were sparkling upon her arms and the clasp seemed to contain her portrait; a string of beautiful pearls encircled her throat.

A lark now commenced its song just above the lovely little girl and awakened her from her profound slumber. She looked about her, called her nurse but finding herself alone in the woods, began to weep bitterly.

Ourson was much affected at her tears and his embarrassment was very great.

"If I show myself," said he to himself, "this poor little

one will take me for some wild beast of the forest. If she sees me she will be terrified; she will take to flight and wander still further from her home. If I leave her here, she will die of terror and hunger. What shall I do!"

Whilst Ourson reflected thus, the little girl turned around, saw him, uttered a cry of alarm, tried to flee and fell back in a panic.

"Do not fly from me, dear little one," said Ourson, in his sad, soft voice; "I would not injure you for the whole world; on the contrary, I will assist you to find your father and mother."

The child gazed at him with staring eyes and seemed much alarmed.

"Speak to me, little one," said Ourson; "I am not a bear, as you might suppose, but a poor and most unfortunate little boy, who inspires every one with terror and whom everybody avoids."

The sweet child's eyes became calmer and softer, her fear seemed melting away and she looked undecided.

Ourson took one step towards her but she became greatly frightened, uttered a sharp cry and tried again to rise and run off. Ourson paused and began to weep bitterly.

"Unfortunate wretch that I am," he said; "I cannot even assist this poor lost child. My appearance fills her with terror! She would rather be lost than have help from me!"

So saying, poor Ourson covered his face with his hands

and sobbing piteously threw himself on the ground. A few moments afterwards he felt a little hand seeking to take possession of his own. He raised his head and saw the child standing before him, her eyes filled with tears. She caressed and patted the hairy cheeks of poor Ourson.

"Don't cry, little cub, don't cry," said she. "Violette is no longer afraid, she will not run away again. Violette will love poor little cub. Won't little cub give his hand to Violette? And if you cry again, Violette will embrace you, poor little cub."

Tears of happiness and tenderness succeeded those of despair in Ourson. Violette, seeing that he was again weeping, approached her soft rosy lips to Ourson's hairy cheek and gave him several kisses.

"You see, little cub, that Violette is no longer afraid. Violette kisses you! The little cub won't eat Violette—she will follow you!"

If Ourson had followed the dictates of his heart, he would have pressed her to his bosom and covered with kisses the good and charming child who overcame her natural terror in order to assuage the grief and mortification of a poor being whom she saw unfortunate and miserable. But he feared to arouse her terrors.

"She would think that I was about to devour her," he said.

He contented himself, therefore, with clasping her

hands softly, and kissing them delicately. Violette permitted this smilingly.

"Now little cub is satisfied. Little cub will love Violette; poor Violette, who is lost!"

Ourson understood well that her name was Violette; but he could not comprehend how this little girl, so richly clad, was left alone in the forest.

"Where do you live, my dear little Violette?"

"Yonder—yonder—with papa and mamma."

"What is the name of your papa?"

"He is the king and dear mamma is the queen."

Ourson was more and more surprised and asked:

"Why are you alone in this forest?"

"Violette doesn't know. Poor Violette rode on a big dog—he ran, oh! so fast—so fast, a long time! Violette was so tired, she fell down and slept!"

"And the dog, where is he?"

Violet turned in every direction and called softly:

"Ami! Ami!"

No dog appeared.

"Alas! Ami has gone! Poor Violette is alone—alone!"

Ourson took Violette's hand and she did not withdraw it but smiled sweetly.

"Shall I go and seek mamma, Violette?"

"No, no! Violette cannot stay all alone in this wood. Violette will go."

"Come, then, with me, dear little girl. I will take you to my mother."

Ourson and Violette now turned their steps towards the farm. Ourson gathered strawberries and cherries for Violette, who would not touch them till Ourson had eaten half. When she found that he still held his half in his hand, she took them, and placed them herself in his mouth, saying:

"Eat—eat, little cub. Violette will not eat unless you eat. Violette cannot have little cub unhappy. Violette will not see you weep."

She looked at him to see if he was content and happy. Ourson was really happy. He saw that his good and pretty little companion not only tolerated him but was interested in him and sought to make herself agreeable. His eyes were sparkling with joy, his voice, always soft and sad, was now tender. After half an hour's walk, he said to her:

"Violette, you are no longer afraid of poor Ourson, are you?"

"Oh! no, no, no!" exclaimed she. "Ourson is good—Violette will not leave him."

"You are willing, then, that I shall embrace you? you are no longer afraid of me?"

Violette, without further reply, threw herself in his arms. Ourson embraced her tenderly and pressed her to his heart.

"Dear Violette, I will always love you. I will never

forget that you are the only child who was ever willing to speak to me, touch me or embrace me."

A short time after they arrived at the farm. Agnella and Passerose were seated at the door, talking together. When they saw Ourson arrive holding a little girl richly dressed by the hand, they were so surprised that neither could utter a word.

"Dear mamma, here is a good and charming little girl whom I found sleeping in the forest. She is called Violette. She is very well bred and is not afraid of me. She even embraced me when she saw me weeping."

"And why did you weep, my poor boy?" said Agnella.

"Because the little girl was afraid of me," said Ourson, in a sad and trembling voice, "and hurt herself when trying to run away from me."

"Violette is not afraid now," said she, interrupting him hastily. "Violette gave her hand to poor Ourson, embraced him and fed him with cherries and strawberries."

"But what is all this about?" said Passerose. "Why has our Ourson the charge of this little girl? why was she alone in the wood? who is she? Answer, Ourson, I do not understand this."

"I know nothing more than yourself, dear Passerose," said Ourson. "I saw this little child asleep in the wood all alone. She awoke and began to weep. Suddenly she saw me and cried out in terror. I spoke to her and began to approach her; but she screamed again with fright. I was sorrowful—oh! so very sorrowful! I wept bitterly."

"Hush! hush! poor Ourson," exclaimed Violette, putting her little hand on his mouth; "Violette will certainly never make you cry again."

While saying these words Violette's voice was trembling and her sweet eyes were full of tears.

"Good little girl!" said Agnella, embracing her; "you love our poor Ourson, who is so unhappy!"

"Oh, yes! Violette loves Ourson—will always love Ourson!"

Agnella and Passerose asked Violette many questions about her father, mother and country; but they could learn nothing more from her than she had already told Ourson. Her father was a king, her mother a queen and she did not know how she came to be alone in the forest.

Agnella did not hesitate to take under her protection this poor lost child. She loved her already because of the affection the little one seemed to entertain for Ourson and because of the happiness Ourson's whole manner expressed on seeing himself loved by some one else than his mother and Passerose.

It was now the hour for supper. Passerose laid the cloth and they all took their seats at the table. Violette asked to be put at Ourson's side. She was gay and laughed and talked merrily. Ourson was more happy than he had ever been. Agnella was contented and Passerose jumped for joy on seeing a little playmate for her dear Ourson. In her transports she spilled a pan of cream which was not lost, however, as a cat came and licked it up to the last drop. After supper, Violette fell asleep in her chair.

"Where shall we lay her?" said Agnella. "I have no bed for her."

"Give her mine, dear mamma," said Ourson; "I can sleep quite as well in the stable."

Agnella and Passerose at first refused but Ourson insisted so much upon being allowed to make this little sacrifice, that they at last consented. Passerose carried Violette still sleeping in her arms, undressed her without awaking her and laid her quietly in Ourson's bed, near that of Agnella. Ourson went to sleep in the stable on the bundles of hay. He slept peacefully with content in his heart.

Passerose rejoined Agnella in the parlor. She found her meditating, with her head resting on her hand.

"Of what are you thinking, dear queen?" said she; "your eyes are sad, your lips do not smile. I am come to show you the bracelets of the little stranger. This medallion ought to open but I have tried in vain to open it. Perhaps we shall find here a portrait or a name."

"Give it to me, my child. These bracelets are beautiful; they may aid us, perhaps, in finding a resemblance which presents itself vaguely to my remembrance and which I am trying in vain to make clear."

Agnella took the bracelets and turned them from side to side and pressed them in every way, trying to open the medallion, but she succeeded no better than Passerose had done.

At the moment when, weary of her vain efforts, she returned them to Passerose, she saw in the middle of the room a woman glittering as the sun; her face was of dazzling whiteness, her hair seemed made of threads of gold and a crown of glittering stars adorned her brow. Her waist was small and her person seemed transparent, it was so delicate and luminous; her floating robe was studded with stars like those which formed her crown. Her glance was soft yet she smiled maliciously but still with goodness.

"Madam," said she to Agnella, "you see in me the fairy Drolette, the protectress of your son and of the little princess whom he brought home this morning from the forest. This princess is nearly related to you for she is your niece—the daughter of your brother-in-law Indolent and sister-in-law Nonchalante. Your husband succeeded after your flight in killing Indolent and Nonchalante, who did not distrust him and who passed all their time in sleeping, eating and lounging. Unfortunately, I could not prevent this crime as I was absent assisting at the birth of a prince whose parents are under my protection, and I forgot myself while playing tricks upon a wicked old maid of honor and an old chamberlain who was cruel and avaricious, both of them friends of my sister, the fairy Furious. But I arrived in time to save the princess Violette, only daughter and heiress of King Indolent and Queen Nonchalante. She was playing in the garden while the king Ferocious was seeking her with his poniard in his hand. I induced her to mount on the back of my dog Ami, who was ordered to leave her in the forest and to that point I directed the steps of the prince your son. Conceal from both of them their birth and your own and do not allow Violette to see these bracelets, which contain the portraits of her father and mother, nor the rich clothing which I have replaced by other articles better suited to the quiet existence she will lead here. I have here," said the fairy, "a casket of precious stones. It contains the happiness of Violette but you must hide them from all eyes and not open the casket until she shall have been lost and found."

"I will execute your orders most faithfully, madam, but I pray you tell me if my unhappy son must long wear his frightful covering."

"Patience! patience!" cried the fairy, "I watch over you, over Violette and over your son. Inform Ourson of the faculty he has of exchanging his skin with any one who loves him well enough to make this sacrifice for his sake. Remember that no one must know the rank of Ourson or of Violette. Passerose, on account of devotion, deserves to be the only one initiated into this mystery and she can always be trusted. Adieu, queen; count always upon my protection. Here is a ring, which you must place upon your little finger. As long as you wear it there you will want for nothing."

Waving her farewell with her hand, the fairy took the form of a lark and flew away singing merrily.

Agnella and Passerose looked at each other. Agnella sighed, Passerose smiled.

"Let us hide this precious casket, dear queen, and the clothing of Violette. I am going now to see what the fairy has prepared for Violette's dress to-morrow morning."

She ran quickly and opened the wardrobe, and found it filled with clothing, linen and hosiery, all plain but good and comfortable. After having looked at all, counted all and approved all and after having assisted Agnella to undress, Passerose went to bed and was soon sound asleep.

THE DREAM

IN the morning Ourson was the first awake, aroused by the lowing of the cow. He rubbed his eyes and looked about him and asked himself why he was in a stable. Then he recalled the events of the day before, sprang up from his bundle of hay and ran quickly to the fountain to wash his face.

While he was washing, Passerose, who had like Ourson risen at a very early hour and had come out to milk the cow, left the house-door open. Ourson entered quietly and proceeded to the chamber of his mother, who was still sleeping. He drew back the curtains from Violette's bed and found her sleeping as peacefully as Agnella.

Ourson watched her for a long time and was happy to see that she smiled in her dreams. Suddenly Violette's brow contracted and she uttered a cry of alarm, half raised herself in the bed, and throwing her little arms around Ourson's neck, she exclaimed:

"Ourson! good Ourson! save poor Violette! poor Violette is in the water and a wicked toad is pulling Violette!"

She now awoke, weeping bitterly, with all the symptoms of great alarm. She clasped Ourson tightly with her little arms; he tried in vain to reassure and control her but she still exclaimed:

"Wicked toad! good Ourson! save Violette!"

Agnella, who had awaked at her first cry, could not yet understand Violette's alarm but she succeeded at last in calming her and the child told her dream.

"Violette was walking with Ourson but he did not give his hand to Violette nor look at her. A wicked toad came and pulled Violette into the water; she fell and called Ourson; he came and saved Violette. She loves good Ourson," she added, in a tender voice; "will never forget him."

Saying these words, Violette threw herself into his arms. He, no longer fearing the effect of his bear-skin, embraced her a thousand times and comforted and encouraged her.

Agnella had no doubt that this dream was a warning sent by the fairy Drolette. She resolved to watch carefully over Violette and to make known to Ourson all that she could reveal to him without disobeying the fairy.

When she had washed and dressed Violette, she called Ourson to breakfast. Passerose brought them a bowl of milk fresh from the cow, some good brown bread and a pot of butter. Violette, who was hungry, shouted for joy when she saw this good breakfast.

"Violette loves good milk, good bread, good butter, loves everything here, with good Ourson and good Mamma Ourson!"

"I am not called Mamma Ourson," said Agnella, laughing; "call me only Mamma."

"Oh no, no! not mamma!" cried Violette, shaking her head sadly. "Mamma! mamma is lost! she was always sleeping, never walking, never taking care of poor Violette, never kissing little Violette, Mamma Ourson speaks, walks, kisses Violette and dresses her. I love Mamma Ourson, oh, so much!" she said, seizing Agnella's hand and pressing it to her heart.

Agnella replied by clasping her tenderly in her arms.

Ourson was much moved—his eyes were moist. Violette perceived this and passing her hand over his eyes, she said, entreatingly:

"I pray you don't cry, Ourson; if you cry, Violette must cry too."

"No, no, dear little girl, I will cry no more. Let us eat our breakfast and then we will take a walk."

They breakfasted with good appetites. Violette clapped her hands frequently and exclaimed:

"Oh how good it is! I love it! I am very glad!"

After breakfast, Ourson and Violette went out to walk

while Agnella and Passerose attended to the house. Ourson played with Violette and gathered her flowers and strawberries. She said to him:

"We will always walk with each other. You must always play with Violette."

"I cannot always play, little girl. I have to help mamma and Passerose to work."

"What sort of work, Ourson?"

"To sweep, scour, take care of the cow, cut the grass and bring wood and water."

"Violette will work with Ourson."

"You are too little, dear Violette, but still you can try."

When they returned to the house, Ourson started on his various tasks. Violette followed him everywhere, she did her best and believed that she was helping him but she was really too small to be useful. After some days had passed away, she began to wash the cups and saucers, spread the cloth, fold the linen and wipe the table. She went to the milking with Passerose, helped to strain the milk and skim it and wash the marble flag-stones. She was never out of temper, never disobedient and never answered impatiently or angrily.

Ourson loved her more and more from day to day. Agnella and Passerose were also very fond of her and the more so because they knew that she was Ourson's cousin.

Violette loved them but Ourson most of all. How

could she help loving this good boy, who always forgot himself for her, who was constantly seeking to amuse and please her and who would indeed have been willing to die for his little friend?

One day, when Passerose had taken Violette with her to market, Agnella related to Ourson the sad circumstances which had preceded his birth. She revealed to him the possibility of his getting rid of his hairy skin and receiving a smooth white skin in exchange if he could ever find any one who would voluntarily make this sacrifice from affection and gratitude.

"Never," cried Ourson, "never will I propose or accept such a sacrifice. I will never consent to devote a being who loves me to that life of wretchedness which the vengeance of the fairy Furious has condemned me to endure; never, from a wish of mine, shall a heart capable of such a sacrifice suffer all that I have suffered and all that I still suffer from the fear and antipathy of men."

Agnella argued in vain against this firm and noble resolve of Ourson. He declared that she must never again speak to him of this exchange, to which he would most assuredly never give his consent and that it must never be named to Violette or any other person who loved him.

Agnella promised compliance, after a few weak arguments. In reality she approved and admired his sentiments. She could not but hope, however, that the fairy Drolette would recompense the generous and noble character of her little charge and, by some extraordinary exercise of her power, release him from his hairy skin.

THE TOAD AGAIN

SOME years passed away in this peaceful manner without the occurrence of any remarkable event. Ourson and Violette both grew rapidly. Agnella thought no more of Violette's frightful dream; her vigilance had greatly relaxed and she often allowed her to walk alone or under the care of Ourson.

Ourson was now fifteen years of age and he was tall and strong. No one could say whether he was handsome or homely for his long black hair covered his body and face entirely. He was good, generous and loving—always ready to render a service, always contented and cheerful. Since the day when he had found Violette in the wood his melancholy had disappeared; he was utterly indifferent to the general antipathy which he inspired and he no longer walked in uninhabited places but lived happily in the circle of the three beings whom he cherished and who loved him supremely.

Violette was now ten years old and she had not lost a single sweet charm of her beauty in growing up. Her eyes were softer and more angelic, her complexion fresher and purer, her mouth more beautiful and arch in its expression. She had grown much in height—was tall, light and graceful and her rich blonde hair, when unbound, fell to her feet and entirely enveloped her like a veil. Passerose had the care of this superb hair and Agnella never ceased to admire it.

Violette had learned many things during those seven years. Agnella had taught her how to do housework. In other things, Ourson had been her teacher. He had taught her to read, write and keep accounts and he often read aloud to her while she was sewing. Instructive and amusing books were found in her room without any one knowing where they came from. There was also clothing and other necessary objects for Violette, Ourson, Agnella and Passerose. There was no longer any necessity for going to market to sell or the neighboring village to buy. Through the agency of the ring on Agnella's little finger everything they wished for, or had need of, was speedily brought to them.

One day when Ourson was walking with Violette she stumbled against a stone, fell and hurt her foot. Ourson was frightened when he saw his cherished Violette bleeding. He did not know what to do to relieve her; he saw how much she suffered, for, notwithstanding all her efforts, she could not suppress the tears which escaped from her eyes but finally he remembered that a brook flowed not ten paces from them.

"Dear Violette," he said, "lean upon me and we will endeavor to reach the rivulet—the fresh water will relieve you."

Violette tried to walk while Ourson supported her. He succeeded in seating her on the borders of the stream where she took off her shoe and bathed her delicate little foot in the fresh flowing water.

"I will run to the house, dear Violette, and bring some linen to wrap up your foot. Wait for me, I shall not be long absent and take good care not to get nearer the stream for this little brook is deep and if you slip you might drown."

When Ourson was out of sight Violette felt an uneasiness which she attributed to the pain caused by her wound. An unaccountable repulsion made her feel inclined to withdraw her foot from the water in which it was hanging. Before she decided to obey this strange impulse she saw the water troubled and the head of an enormous toad appear upon the surface. The great swollen angry eyes of the loathsome animal were fixed upon Violette, who since her dream had always had a dread of toads. The appearance of this hideous creature, its monstrous swollen body and menacing glance, froze her with such horror that she could neither move nor cry out.

"Ah! ha! you are at last in my domain, little fool!" said the toad. "I am the fairy Furious, the enemy of your family. I have been lying in wait for you a long time and should have had you before if my sister, the fairy Drolette, had not protected you and sent you a dream to warn you against me. Ourson whose hairy skin is a talisman of safety is now absent, my sister is on a journey and you are at last mine."

Saying these words, she seized Violette's foot with her cold and shining paws and tried to draw her down into the water. Violette uttered the most piercing shrieks; she struggled and caught hold of the plants and shrubs growing on the borders of the stream. The first, alas, gave way, and Violette in despair seized hold of others.

"Ourson! oh, Ourson! help! help! dear Ourson, save me, save your poor Violette! I am perishing! save me! help! help!"

The fairy Furious, in the form of a toad, was about to carry her off. The last shrub had given way and Violette's last cry was hushed.

The poor Violette disappeared under the water just as another cry, more despairing, more terrible, answered to her own. But, alas! her hair alone appeared above the water when Ourson reached the spot, breathless and panting with terror. He had heard Violette's cries and had turned back with the rapidity of lightning.

Without a moment's hesitation he sprang into the water and seized Violette by her long hair but he felt instantly that he was sinking with her. The fairy Furious was drawing them to the bottom of the stream. He knew he was sinking but he did not lose his self-possession. Instead of releasing Violette, he seized her both arms and invoked the fairy Drolette. When they reached the bottom, he gave one vigorous stroke with his heel which brought him again to the surface. Holding Violette securely with one arm, he swam sturdily with the other and through some supernatural force he reached the shore where he deposited the unconscious Violette.

Her eyes were closed, her teeth tightly clenched and the pallor of death was on her face. Ourson threw himself on his knees by her side weeping bitterly. Brave Ourson, whom no dangers could intimidate, no privation, no suffering could master, now wept like a child. His sweet sister, so well beloved! his only friend, his consolation, his happiness was lying there motionless, lifeless! Ourson's strength and courage had deserted him and he sank down without consciousness by the side of his beloved Violette.

At this moment a lark flew rapidly up, approached Violette and Ourson, gave one stroke of her little beak to Ourson and another to Violette and disappeared.

Ourson was not the only one who replied to the shrieks of Violette. Passerose had heard them and then the more terrible cry of Ourson which succeeded them. She ran to the house to apprise Agnella and they both ran rapidly toward the stream from which the cries for help seemed to come.

On approaching, they saw with surprise and alarm that Violette and Ourson were lying on the ground in a state of unconsciousness. Passerose placed her hand on Violette's heart and felt it still beating. Agnella ascertained at the same moment that Ourson was still living. She directed Passerose to take Violette home, undress her and put her to bed while she endeavored to restore consciousness to Ourson with salts and other restoratives before conducting him to the farm. Ourson was too tall and heavy to be carried while Violette, on the contrary, was light and it was easy for Passerose to carry her to the house. When she arrived there, she was soon restored to animation. It was some moments before she was conscious. She was still agitated with a vague remembrance of terror but without knowing what had alarmed her.

During this time the tender care of Agnella had restored Ourson to life. He opened his eyes, gazed tenderly at his mother and threw himself weeping upon her neck.

"Mother, dear mother!" he exclaimed, "my Violette, my beloved sister, has perished! Let me die with her!"

"Be composed, my son," replied Agnella; "Violette still lives. Passerose has carried her to the house and will bestow upon her all the attention she requires."

Ourson seemed to revive on hearing these words. He rose and wished to run to the farm but his second thought was consideration for his mother and he restrained his impatience to suit her steps. On their way to the farm he told his mother all that he knew of the events which had almost cost Violette and himself their lives. He added that the slime from the mouth of the fairy Furious had left a strange dulness in his head.

Agnella now told him how Passerose and herself had found them stretched unconscious upon the border of the stream. They soon arrived at the farm, and Ourson, still dripping, rushed into Violette's presence.

On seeing him Violette remembered everything and she sprang towards him. She threw her arms around him and wept upon his bosom. Ourson also wept and Agnella and Passerose were both in tears. It was a concert of emotion, enough to soften all hearts. Passerose put an end to it by crying out:

"Would not one say—ha! ha!—that we were the most—ha! ha!—unfortunate people—ha! ha!—in the universe!—Look at our poor Ourson, wet as a water-reed, bathing himself in his own and Violette's tears. Courage, children, courage and happiness! See, we are all alive, thanks to Ourson."

"Oh, yes!" interrupted Violette; "thanks to Ourson—to my dear, my well-beloved Ourson. How shall I ever repay him for all I owe him? How can I ever testify my profound gratitude, my tender affection?"

"By loving me always as you do now, my dear Violette, my sister. Ah! if it has indeed been in my power to render you some little service, have you not changed my whole existence? Have you not made me gay and happy—me who was so wretched and so miserable before? Are you not every day and every hour of the day the consolation and happiness of my life and of that of my excellent mother?"

Violette was still weeping and she answered only by pressing more tenderly to her heart her Ourson, her adopted brother.

"Dear son," said his mother, "you are dripping wet. Go and change your clothing. Violette has need of some hours' repose. We will meet again at dinner."

Violette consented to go to bed but did not sleep for her heart was melting, overflowing with gratitude and tenderness. She sought in vain for some means of rewarding the devotion of Ourson. She could think of no other way than that of trying to become perfect so as to increase the happiness of Ourson and Agnella.

VIOLETTE'S SACRIFICE

WHEN the dinner hour came, Violette arose, dressed herself and entered the dining-room where Agnella and Passerose were awaiting her. Ourson was not there.

"Ourson is not with you, mother," said Violette.

"I have not seen him," said Agnella.

"Nor I," said Passerose; "I will go and seek him."

She entered his chamber and found him seated upon his bed, his head resting upon his arm.

"Come, Ourson, come quick; we are waiting dinner for you."

"I cannot come," said Ourson, in a weak voice; "I have a strange heaviness in my head."

Passerose flew to inform Agnella and Violette of his illness and they were by his side in an instant. Ourson made an effort to rise in order to reassure them but he fell upon a chair. Agnella found that he had a violent fever and she prevailed upon him to lie down. Violette absolutely refused to leave him.

"I am the cause of his illness," she said, "and I will not leave his side till he is well. I shall die of anxiety if you force me to leave my dear brother."

Agnella and Passerose also installed themselves near their dear invalid but alas! soon poor Ourson did not recognise them. He was delirious! He called his mother and Violette every moment and continued to call them most importunately and to complain of their absence, even while they were holding him in their arms.

Agnella and Violette never left him day nor night during all his sickness. The eighth day, Agnella, exhausted with fatigue, had fallen asleep near the poor sufferer's bed; his difficult respiration and lifeless eye seemed to announce the near approach of death. Violette was on her knees, holding and pressing in her fine white hands the hairy hands of Ourson and covering them with tears and kisses.

In the midst of this scene of desolation, a clear sweet song interrupted the mournful silence of the chamber of the dying boy. Violette started. This soft melody seemed to bring consolation and happiness; she raised her head and saw a lark perched upon the open shutter.

"Violette!" said the lark.

Violette trembled fearfully.

"Violette," repeated the little soft voice of the lark, "do you love Ourson?"

"Do I love him? Ah! love him—I love him more than any one else—more than I love myself."

"Would you purchase his life at the price of your happiness?"

"Yes, gladly would I purchase life for him by the sacrifice of my happiness and of my own life."

"Listen, then, Violette. I am the fairy Drolette. I love Ourson, I love you and I love your family. The venom which my sister the fairy Furious has blown upon the head of Ourson is sufficient to cause his death. Nevertheless, if you are sincere, if you really feel for Ourson the sentiments of gratitude and tenderness which you express, his life is in your hands. You are permitted to redeem it! But remember that you will soon be called upon to give the most terrible proof of your attachment and that if he lives you will pay for his existence by a most horrible sacrifice."

"Oh, madam! quick, quick, tell me what I am to do to save my dear Ourson. Nothing will be terrible to me, all will be joy and happiness if you aid me to save my brother Ourson."

"Well, my child, very well," replied the fairy. "Kiss his left ear three times, saying at each kiss: *'To thee!—For thee! —With thee!'* Reflect again, Violette, before undertaking this cure. If you are not prepared for the most difficult sacrifices, the greatest misfortunes will overwhelm you and my sister Furious will be the mistress of your life."

As her only reply, Violette crossed her hands upon her breast, cast upon the fairy, who was about to fly away, a look of tender gratitude, and, throwing herself upon Ourson, she kissed his left ear three times, saying, with an accent loving and penetrating:

"To thee!—For thee!—With thee!"

Scarcely had she said these words, when Ourson uttered a profound sigh, opened his eyes, perceived Violette and seizing her hands carried them to his lips, saying:

"Violette, dear Violette! it seems to me I am awaking from a long dream. Tell me all that has passed. Why am I here? Why are you so pale and thin? Your cheeks are hollow, you seem to have grown old and your beautiful eyes are red with weeping."

"Hush!" said Violette, "do not wake your mother, who is sleeping by your side. She has not slept for a long time and is much fatigued. You have been very ill, Ourson!"

"And you, dear Violette, have you been resting?"

Violette blushed and hesitated.

"How could I sleep, dear Ourson, when I was the cause of all your sufferings?"

Ourson was silent. He looked at her tenderly, kissed her hands and again asked her to tell him what had passed. She told him but she was too modest and too truly devoted to reveal to him the price that the fairy had affixed to his cure. Ourson, therefore, was far from knowing the truth.

Ourson now felt himself restored to health, rose up, proceeded to his mother softly and awakened her by a kiss. Agnella thought he was delirious and called Passerose who was astonished when Violette told them that Ourson had been restored by the good fairy Drolette.

After all this, Ourson and Violette loved each other more tenderly than ever and they never left each other unless their occupations forced them to be apart.

THE WILD BOAR

TWO years passed. One day Ourson had been cutting wood in the forest. Violette was to bring him his dinner and return with him in the evening. At midday Passerose hung on Violette's arm a basket containing wine, bread, a little pot of butter, some ham and some cherries. Violette set off eagerly. The morning had appeared to her very long and she was impatient to be again with Ourson. To shorten the way she went through the forest which was composed of large trees under which she could easily walk. There were neither briars nor thorns in her way and a soft, thick moss covered the earth.

Violette stepped lightly for she was happy to have found a shorter path to her dear Ourson. When she had passed over about half the distance she heard the noise of a heavy and precipitate step but too far off for her to imagine what it could be. After some moments of expectation she saw an enormous wild boar coming towards her. He seemed greatly enraged, ploughed the ground with his tusks and rubbed the bark from the trees as he passed along. His heavy snorting and breathing were as distinctly heard as his step. Violette did not know where to fly or to hide herself. While she was hesitating the wild boar came in sight, saw her, and paused. His eyes were flaming, his whole body bristling, his tusks clashing together. He uttered a ferocious grunt, and sprang towards Violette. Happily she was near a tree whose branches were within her reach. She seized one, sprang up with it, and climbed from branch to branch, until she knew she was beyond his reach. Scarcely was she in safety when the savage animal precipitated himself with all his weight against the tree in which she had taken refuge. Furious at this obstacle, he commenced tearing the bark from the tree and gave it such furious blows with his snout that Violette was terribly frightened. The concussion caused by these violent and repeated blows might at last cause the fall of the tree. She clung tightly and trembling to the tree. The wild boar at last weary of his useless attacks laid himself down at the foot of the tree casting from time to time a menacing look at Violette.

Many hours passed in this painful situation, Violette trembling but holding on steadily and the wild boar, sometimes calm, sometimes in a terrible rage, springing against the tree and tearing it with his tusks.

Violette takes refuge from the wild boar

Violette called on her brother, her dear Ourson, for help. At every new attempt of the wild boar she renewed her cries for aid but alas! Ourson was too far off and he could not hear. No one came to her aid.

Discouragement and despair gained upon her; she began to feel hunger. She had thrown away the basket of provisions when she sprang up the tree, the wild boar had trampled upon it, crushed it and eaten up everything it contained.

Whilst Violette was a prey to these terrors and vainly calling for help Ourson was amazed at not seeing her come with the dinner.

"Can they have forgotten me?" he said to himself. "No, neither my mother nor Violette could have forgotten me. I could not have explained myself well. Without doubt they expected me back to dinner; they are looking for me now and are perhaps uneasy."

At this thought Ourson abandoned his work and commenced walking precipitately towards the house. He also wished to shorten the way and determined to cross the forest. Soon he thought he heard plaintive cries of distress. He paused—he listened, his heart beat violently as he believed he recognized the voice of Violette. But, no—he heard nothing now. He was about to resume his march when he heard a more distinct and piercing cry.

Now he knew that it must be Violette, his Violette, who was in danger and calling upon Ourson for help. He ran in the direction from which the noise seemed to come. Approaching, he heard not only calls for help but roars and growls accompanied by ferocious cries and violent blows. Poor Ourson ran on with the speed of despair. At last he perceived the wild boar shaking with his snout the tree upon which Violette was still crouched in safety though pale and overcome.

This sight gave him new strength. He invoked the protection of the good fairy Drolette and rushed upon the wild boar with his axe in his hand. The wild boar in his rage bellowed furiously. He gnashed his formidable tusks one against the other and sprang towards Ourson, who dodged the attack and jumped to one side. The boar passed beyond him, paused a moment, then turned more furious than ever against Ourson who had now taken breath and with his axe raised in his hand awaited his enemy.

The wild boar sprung on Ourson and received on his head a most violent blow but his bones were so hard he scarcely seemed to feel it. The violence of the attack overthrew Ourson. The wild boar, seeing his enemy on the ground, did not give him time to rise but sprang upon him and with his tusks endeavored to tear him to pieces.

Ourson now thought himself lost, indeed he thought no more of himself, he prayed only for Violette's safety.

Whilst the wild boar was thus trampling and kicking his enemy, a jeering song was heard just above the combatants. The wild boar shuddered, suddenly quitted Ourson, raised his head and saw a lark flying above them. The mocking song continued and the brute, uttering a cry of rage, lowered his head and withdrew slowly without once turning round.

Violette at sight of Ourson's danger had fainted away but had rested supported by the branches of the tree. Ourson, who thought himself torn to pieces, scarcely dared attempt to move but feeling no pain he rose promptly to assist Violette. His heart was full of gratitude to the fairy Drolette to whom he attributed his rescue. At this moment the lark flew towards him, pecked his cheeks and whispered in his ear:

"Ourson, it was the fairy Furious who sent this wild boar. I arrived in time to save you. Profit by the gratitude of Violette and change skins with her. She will consent joyfully."

"Never!" cried Ourson. "I would rather be a bear all my life—rather die. Poor Violette! I should indeed be base if I abused her tenderness towards me in this way."

"Good-bye, obstinate one!" said the lark, flying away singing, "till we meet again. I shall come again—and then——"

"The result will be the same," said Ourson.

He then climbed the tree, took Violette in his arms, and descended. He laid her upon the soft green moss and bathed her forehead with a little wine he found in a broken bottle.

In a few moments Violette was restored to consciousness. She could scarcely believe her senses when she saw Ourson, living and unwounded, kneeling by her side and bathing her forehead and temples.

"Ourson! dear Ourson! again you have saved my life. Tell me, oh! tell me, what can I do to prove my gratitude?"

"Do not speak of gratitude, my cherished Violette. Do I not owe all my happiness to you? In saving your life I save my own and all I value."

"All that you say, dear brother, is sweet and tender but I desire no less to render you some real and signal service, which will show all the gratitude and all the love with which my heart is filled."

"Good! good! we shall see," said Ourson, laughing. "In the mean time let us think of preserving our lives. You have eaten nothing since morning, poor Violette for I see on the ground the remnants of the provisions you brought, as I suppose, for our dinner. It is late and the day is declining so we must hurry to return to the farm before dark."

Violette now tried to rise but her terror and her long fast had weakened her so much that she fell to the ground.

"I cannot stand, Ourson, I am too weak. What will become of us?"

Ourson was greatly embarrassed. Violette was no longer a child and had grown so large that he could not carry her so far, neither could he leave her exposed to the attacks of the ferocious beasts of the forest and he feared she could not do without food till the morning. In this perplexity he saw a packet fall at his feet. He raised it, opened it and found a pie, a loaf of bread and a bottle of wine. Ourson knew that this bounty was from the hand of the fairy Drolette and with a heart full of gratitude he put the bottle to Vio-

VIOLETTE CONSENTED WILLINGLY TO PASS THE NIGHT IN THE FOREST

—*Page 229*

lette's lips. One mouthful of this good wine which was indeed unequalled restored a portion of Violette's strength. The pie and the bread completely restored her as well as Ourson who did full honor to the repast. While eating and drinking they conversed of their past terrors and present happiness.

Now, however, it was night and neither Violette nor Ourson knew which way to turn their steps in order to reach the farm. They were in the midst of a wood. Violette was reclining against the tree which had been her refuge from the wild boar. They dared not quit this spot lest in the obscurity they might not find as comfortable a one.

"Well, dear Violette, do not be alarmed. It is warm, the weather is beautiful and you are reclining upon a bed of soft green moss. Let us pass the night where we are. I will cover you with my coat and I will lie at your feet to protect you from all danger and alarm. Mamma and Passerose will not be very anxious for they are ignorant of the dangers we have encountered and you know that we have often on a lovely evening like this reached home after they had retired."

Violette consented willingly to pass the night in the forest. In the first place, they could not do otherwise; secondly, she was never afraid with Ourson and always thought that what he decided to do was right.

Ourson now arranged Violette's bed of moss in the best possible manner, took off his coat and in spite of her resistance spread it over her. Then, after having seen Violette's eyes close and sleep take possession of all her senses he lay at her feet and soon slept most profoundly.

Violette was the first awake in the morning. She walked around the tree which had sheltered them during the night. Ourson awaked and not seeing Violette he sprang up in an instant and called her name in a voice choking with terror.

"I am here! I am here, dear brother!" she replied, running towards him; "I am seeking the path to the farm. But what is the matter? you tremble!"

"I thought you had been carried away by some wicked fairy, dear Violette, and I reproached myself for having fallen asleep. Let us go now quickly in order to reach home before mamma and Passerose are awake."

Ourson knew the forest well. He soon found the path to the farm and they arrived some moments before Agnella and Passerose awoke. They agreed to conceal from Agnella the dangers to which they had been exposed, to spare her anguish and disquietude for the future. Passerose alone was made the confidant of their dangerous adventures.

THE CONFLAGRATION

OURSON now forbade Violette to go alone in the forest. She was no longer allowed to carry him his dinner so he always returned to the house at midday. Violette never left the farm without Ourson.

Three years after the event in the forest, Ourson saw Violette arise in the morning pale and exhausted. She was seeking him.

"Come, come," she said, drawing him along, "I have something to say—something to relate— Oh, come!"

Ourson was much alarmed and followed her precipitately.

"What is it, dear Violette? For the love of Heaven, speak to me! What can I do for you?"

"Nothing, nothing, dear Ourson; you can do nothing —only listen to me. You remember the dream I had in my childhood, of the toad! the river! the danger! Well, last night I had this same dream again. It is terrible! terrible! Ourson, dear Ourson, your life is menaced! If you die, I will die also!"

"How! By whom is my life threatened?"

"Listen! I was sleeping and a toad—still a toad—always a toad—came to me and said:

" 'The moment approaches when your dear Ourson is to resume his natural skin. To you he is to be indebted for this change. I hate him! I hate you! You shall not make each other happy! Ourson shall perish and you cannot accomplish the sacrifice which in your folly you meditate. In a few days, yes, perhaps in a few hours I shall take a signal vengeance upon you both. Good-bye—do you hear?—till we meet again!'

"I awoke, suppressed a cry which was about to issue from my lips and saw, as I saw on that day in which you saved me from the water, the hideous toad creeping upon the shutter and gazing at me menacingly. It disappeared, leaving me more dead than alive. I arose dressed myself and came to find you my brother, my friend to warn you against the vengeance of the fairy Furious and to entreat you to seek the aid of the good fairy Drolette."

Ourson listened in great alarm. He was not frightened by the fate which menaced himself—he was agitated by the sacrifice which Furious announced and which he understood but too well. The thought alone of his dear and lovely

Violette being muffled up in his hideous bear's skin through devotion to him made him tremble and he preferred death. Ourson's anguish was pictured in his countenance, and Violette, who was watching him closely, threw herself upon his neck and sobbed violently.

"Alas! my brother, my dear brother, you will soon be torn from me. You, who do not know what it is to fear, now tremble. You who comfort me encourage me and sustain me in all my fears have now no word to utter to restore my failing courage. You who have combated the most terrible dangers now bow your head and are resigned to fate."

"No, Violette, it is not fear which makes me tremble—it is not fear which agitates me. It is a word which the fairy Furious has uttered, of which you do not comprehend the meaning but which I understand perfectly. The threat was addressed to you, my Violette. It is for you I tremble!"

Violette divined from this that the moment of sacrifice had come, that she was about to be called upon to keep the promise she had made to the fairy Drolette. In place of trembling and shrinking, she felt the most lively joy. She could now at last make some return for the devotion, the incessant watchful tenderness of her dear Ourson—could in her turn be useful to him. She made no response to the fears expressed by Ourson but thanked him and spoke to him more tenderly than ever before, thinking that soon perhaps she would be separated from him by death. Ourson had the same thought. They both fervently invoked the protection of the fairy Drolette. Ourson, indeed, called upon her in a loud voice but she did not respond to his appeal.

The day passed away sadly. Neither Ourson nor Violette spoke to Agnella on the subject of their disquiet for fear of aggravating her melancholy which had been constantly increasing as Ourson grew to manhood.

"Already twenty years old!" thought she. "If he persists in living in this solitude and seeing no one and in refusing to change with Violette, who asks nothing better, I am certain, I am convinced, he will wear this bear-skin till his death."

Agnella wept, often wept; but her tears brought her no remedy.

The day Violette had her frightful dream, Agnella also had a dream. The fairy Drolette had appeared to her:

"Courage, queen," she said to her, "in a few days Ourson will lose his bear's skin and you can give him his true name of Prince Marvellous."

Agnella had awaked full of hope and happiness. She redoubled her tenderness to Violette, believing that it was to her she would owe the happiness of her son.

Every one retired at night with different feelings. Violette and Ourson, full of anxiety for the future which appeared so threatening, Agnella's heart bounding with joy at that same future which appeared so near and so replete with happiness, Passerose, astonished at the melancholy of the one and the joy of the other and ignorant of the cause of both.

All slept, however. Violette after weeping profusely, Ourson after having invoked the fairy Drolette; Agnella after smiling and thinking of Ourson handsome and attractive and Passerose after saying to herself a hundred times: "But what is the matter with them all to-day?"

Scarcely an hour after all at the farm were asleep, Violette was aroused by the smell of fire and smoke. Agnella awoke at the same moment.

"Mother," said Violette, "do you not smell something?"

"The house is on fire," said Agnella. "Look what a light is round about us!"

They sprang from their beds and ran to the parlor. The flames had already taken possession of it and of the neighboring chambers.

"Ourson! Passerose!" cried Agnella.

"Ourson! Ourson!" exclaimed Violette.

Passerose sprang half clothed into the parlor.

"We are lost, madam! The flames are all through the house. The doors and windows are firmly closed—it is impossible to open them."

"My son! my son!" cried Agnella.

"My brother! my brother!" exclaimed Violette.

They ran to the doors; all their efforts to open them or the windows were ineffectual.

"Oh! my terrible dream!" murmured Violette. "Dear Ourson, adieu for ever!"

Ourson had also been awakened by the flames and smoke. He slept out of the farm-house, and near the stable. His first impulse was to run to the front of the house but notwithstanding his extraordinary strength he could not open it. One would have thought that the door would break to pieces under his efforts. It was evidently held fast by the fairy Furious.

Ourson sprang upon a ladder and passed across the flames into a granary through an open window, then descended into the room where his mother and Violette were embracing, expecting instant death. Before they had time to recognize him he seized them in his arms and cried to Passerose to follow him. He ran along the granary and descended the ladder with his mother in one arm and Violette in the other and followed by Passerose. The moment after they reached the ground in safety, the ladder and granary became a prey to the flames.

Ourson led Agnella and Violette some distance from the fire. Passerose was self-possessed: she had quite a large package of clothing which she had collected at the commencement of the fire. Agnella and Violette had escaped barefooted and in their night robes, and the clothing brought by Passerose was thus very necessary to protect them from the cold. After having thanked Ourson for saving their lives at the peril of his own they complimented Passerose upon her forethought.

"See," said Passerose, "the advantage of not losing one's senses. Whilst you two were only thinking of your Ourson, I made up this package of necessary things."

"That is true, my good Passerose; but what purpose would your package have served, if my mother and Violette had perished in the flames?"

"Oh, I knew very well that you would not allow them to be burned up alive. Is any one ever in danger when you are present? Is not this the third time you have saved Violette's life?"

Violette pressed Ourson's hands tenderly and carried them to her lips. Agnella embraced her and said:

"Dear Violette, Ourson is happy in your tenderness which fully rewards him for all he has done for you. I feel assured that on your part you would be happy to sacrifice yourself for him if an occasion offered, that only too willingly would you help him."

Before Violette could speak, Ourson said with animation:

"Mother, do not say anything to Violette of sacrificing herself for me. You know the thought alone makes me wretched."

In place of replying to Ourson, Agnella placed her hand on her forehead and cried out anxiously:

"The casket, Passerose! the casket! Have you saved the casket?"

"I forgot it, madam," said Passerose.

The countenance of Agnella expressed such regret and anxiety, that Ourson questioned her as to this precious casket which seemed to trouble her so much.

"The casket was a present of the fairy Drolette. She told me that the happiness of Violette was contained in it. It was in the wardrobe, at the foot of my bed. Alas! by what fatality did I forget it?"

She had scarcely uttered these words when the brave Ourson sprang towards the burning house and notwithstanding the tears and supplications of Agnella, Violette and Passerose, disappeared in the flames exclaiming:

"You shall have the casket, mother, or I will perish with it!"

A horrible silence followed this act of Ourson. Violette fell on her knees with her arms extended towards the burning house, Agnella with her hands clasped looked with straining eyes at the opening through which Ourson had entered while Passerose was motionless, hiding her face with her hands. Some moments passed thus and they appeared ages to the three women who were expecting a sentence of life or death.

Ourson did not reappear. The crackling of the burning wood, the flashing of the flames, increased in violence. Suddenly, a frightful noise made Violette and Agnella utter a cry of despair.

The roof, covered with flames, had fallen in and Ourson was buried under the ruins—crushed by the ruins, consumed by the fire.

The silence of death succeeded this dreadful catastrophe. The flames diminished, then died away—no sound now interrupted the despair of Agnella and Violette.

Violette had fallen into the arms of Agnella and they sobbed thus a long time in silence. Passerose contemplated the smoking ruins and wept. Poor Ourson was buried there a victim of his courage and his devotion! Agnella and Violette still wept bitterly; they appeared neither to hear nor understand what was passing around them.

"Let us leave this place," said Passerose, at last.

Agnella and Violette made no response.

Passerose tried to lead Violette away.

"Come," said she; "come, Violette, let us seek a shelter for the night—the evening fortunately is mild."

"What shelter do I want?" said Violette. "What is the evening to me or the morning? There are no more beautiful days for me! The sun will shine no more but to illumine my despair!"

"But if we remain here weeping we shall die of hunger,

Violette, and in spite of the bitterest grief, we must think of the necessities of life."

"Better to die of hunger than of grief! I will not leave this place where I saw my dear Ourson for the last time—where he perished, a victim of his tenderness for us."

Passerose shrugged her shoulders; she remembered that the stable had not been burned so she ran there with all speed, milked the cow, drank a cupful of milk and tried in vain to make Agnella and Violette do the same.

Agnella rose and said to Violette in a solemn tone:

"Your grief is just, my daughter. Never did a more noble or generous heart beat in a human form than Ourson's and he loved you more than he loved himself—to spare your grief he sacrificed his happiness and his life."

Agnella now recounted to Violette the scene which preceded Ourson's birth, the power Violette had to deliver him from his deformity by accepting it for herself and Ourson's constant prayer that Violette should never be informed of the possibility of such a sacrifice.

It is easy to comprehend the feelings of loving tenderness and regret which filled the heart of Violette after this confidence and she wept more bitterly than ever.

"And now, my daughter," continued Agnella, "there remains one duty to fulfil, that is to give burial to my son. We must clear away these ruins and remove the ashes and when we have found the remains of our well-beloved Ourson——"

Sobs interrupted her speech; she could say no more.

THE WELL

AGNELLA, Violette and Passerose walked slowly towards the burned walls of the farmhouse. With the courage of despair they removed the smoking ruins. They worked diligently two days before this work was completed. No vestige of poor Ourson appeared and yet they had removed piece by piece, handful by handful, all that covered the site. On removing the last half-burned planks, Violette perceived an aperture, which she quickly enlarged. It was the orifice of a well. Her heart beat violently—a vague hope inspired it.

"Ourson!" cried she, with a faint voice.

"Violette! dear Violette! I am here; I am saved!"

Violette could reply only by a smothered cry; she lost her consciousness and fell into the well which enclosed her dear Ourson. If the good fairy Drolette had not watched over her fall, she would have broken her head and limbs against the sides of the well. But their kind protectress, who had already rendered them so many services, sustained her and she fell safely at Ourson's feet.

Violette soon returned to consciousness. Their happiness was too great to be believed in—to be trusted. They did not cease to give the most tender assurances of affection. And now they were aroused from their ecstasy by the cries of Passerose, who, losing sight of Violette and seeking her amongst the ruins, discovered the open well. Peering into the darkness she saw Violette's white robe and she imagined that the poor girl had thrown herself intentionally into the well and there found the death she sought. Passerose screamed loud enough to destroy her lungs. Agnella came slowly forward to know the cause of this alarm.

"Be silent, Passerose," cried Ourson in a loud voice; "you are frightening our mother. I am in the well with Violette; we are happy and want for nothing."

"Oh blessed news! blessed news!" cried Passerose; "I see them! I see them! Madam, madam, come quickly, quickly! They are here—they are well—they have need of nothing!"

Agnella, pale, and half dead with emotion, listened to Passerose without comprehending her. She fell on her knees and had not strength to rise. But when she heard the voice of her dear Ourson calling to her: "Mother, mother, your poor son Ourson still lives!" she sprang toward the well, and would have precipitated herself within, had not Passerose seized her by the arms and drawn her back suddenly.

"For the love of Ourson, dear queen, do not throw yourself into this hole; you will kill yourself! I will restore Ourson and Violette to you unharmed."

Agnella, trembling with happiness, comprehended the wisdom of the counsel given by Passerose. She remained rooted to the spot but shuddering with agitation while Passerose ran to seek a ladder.

Passerose was absent a long time which was excusable as she was somewhat confused. First she seized a cord, then a pitchfork, then a chair. For an instant she thought of lowering the cow to the bottom of the well so that poor Ourson might have a drink of fresh warm milk. At last she found the ladder before her eyes, almost in her hands, but she had not seen it.

While Passerose was seeking the ladder, Ourson and Violette talked incessantly of their present happiness and the despair and anguish they had endured.

"I passed uninjured through the flames," said Ourson, "and sought groping about for the wardrobe of my mother. The smoke suffocated and blinded me. Then I felt myself raised by the hair and cast to the bottom of this well where you have come to join me, dear Violette.

"In place of finding water, or even moisture here, I felt

at once a sweet, fresh air. A soft carpet was spread on the bottom: you see it is still here. There was from some source sufficient light around me. I found ample provisions at my side. Look at them, Violette, I have not touched them. A few drops of wine was all I could swallow.

"The knowledge of your despair and that of my mother rendered me too unhappy and the fairy Drolette took pity on me. She appeared to me under your form, dear Violette, and I took her for you and sprang forward to seize you in my arms but I embraced only a vague form of air or vapor. I could see her but I could not touch her.

" 'Ourson,' said the fairy, smiling sweetly upon me, 'I have assumed Violette's form to testify my friendship in the most agreeable way. Be comforted; you shall see her to-morrow. She weeps bitterly, because she believes you to be dead but I will send her to you to-morrow. She will make you a visit at the bottom of this well. She will accompany you when you go forth from this tomb and you shall see your mother and the blue heavens and the dazzling sun which neither your mother nor Violette wish to look upon since your loss, but which appeared beautiful to them while you were with them. You will return once more to this well for it contains your happiness.'

" 'My happiness!' I exclaimed to the fairy; 'when I have found my mother and my Violette I shall be in possession of all my happiness.'

" 'Believe implicitly what I say. This well contains your happiness and that of Violette.'

" 'Violette's happiness, madam, is to live with me and my mother.' "

"Ah! you replied well," interrupted Violette. "But what said the fairy?"

" 'I know what I say,' she answered. 'In a few days something will be wanting to complete your happiness. You will find it here. We will meet again, Ourson. Remember what I have said.'

" 'Yes, madam; I hope it will be soon.'

" 'When you see me again, my poor child, you will be scarcely content and then you will wish that you had never seen me. Silence and farewell.'

"She flew away smiling sweetly, leaving behind her a delicious perfume and an atmosphere so soft and heavenly that it diffused a peaceful calm in my heart. I suffered no more—I expected you."

Violette on her part comprehended better than Ourson why the next return of the fairy would be painful to him. Since Agnella had revealed to her in confidence the nature of the sacrifice that she could impose upon herself, she was resolved to accomplish it, in spite of the opposition of Ourson. She thought only of the delight of giving an immense proof of her affection. This hope tempered her joy at having found him.

When Ourson had completed his narrative, they heard the shrill voice of Passerose crying out to them:

"Look, look, my children! the ladder. I will put it down to you. Take care that it does not fall on your heads. You must have some provisions down there; send them up, if you please; we are somewhat destitute above here. For two days I have only had a little milk to drink and a crust. Your mother and Violette have lived upon the air and their tears. Softly! softly! take care not to break the ladder. Madam! madam! here they are: here are Ourson's and Violette's heads.—Good! Step up! There you are!"

Agnella, still pallid and trembling, was immovable as a statue.

After having seen Violette in safety, Ourson sprang from the well and threw himself into his mother's arms. She covered him with tears and kisses and held him a long time clasped to her heart. After having thought him dead during so many painful hours, it seemed a dream to her almost impossible to realize that she was holding him safe once more. Finally Passerose terminated this melting scene by seizing Ourson and saying to him:

"Now it is my turn! I am forgotten, forsooth, because I do not bathe myself in tears; because I keep my head cool and preserve my strength. Was it not Passerose, after all, who got you out of that terrible hole? Speak the truth."

"Yes, yes, my good Passerose! You may believe that I

love you and indeed I thank you for drawing me out of it where, however, I was doing very well after my sweet Violette came down to me."

"But now I think of it," said Passerose, "tell me, Violette, how did you get to the bottom of that well without killing yourself?"

"I did not go down purposely. I fell and Ourson received me in his arms."

"All this is not very clear," said Passerose. "The fairy Drolette had something to do with it."

"Yes, the good and amiable fairy," said Ourson. "She is always counteracting the cruelties of her wicked sister."

While thus talking merrily, their stomachs gave indication that they were suffering for dinner. Ourson had left in the well the provisions furnished by the fairy. The rest of the happy family were still embracing and weeping over past remembrances but Passerose without saying a word descended into the well and remounted with the provisions which she placed on a bundle of straw; she then placed around the table four other bundles of straw for seats.

"Dinner is ready," said she; "come and eat; you all need food. The good queen and Violette will soon fall from exhaustion. Ourson has had a little wine but he has eaten nothing. Here is a pie, a ham, bread and wine. Long life to the good fairy!"

Agnella, Violette and Ourson did not require to be told

a second time but placed themselves gayly at the table. Their appetites were good and the repast excellent. Happiness illuminated every countenance; they talked, laughed, clasped each other's hands and were in paradise.

When dinner was over, Passerose was surprised that the fairy Drolette had not provided for all their wants.

"Look," said she, "the house is in ruins, we are destitute of everything! The stable is our only shelter, the straw our only bed and the provisions I brought up from the well our only food. Formerly everything was provided before we had the time to ask for it."

Agnella looked suddenly at her hand—the ring was no longer there! They must now gain their bread by the sweat of their brows. Ourson and Violette seeing her air of consternation demanded the cause of it.

"Alas! my children, you will no doubt think me very ungrateful to feel disquieted about the future in the midst of our great happiness but I perceive that during the fire I have lost the ring given me by the good fairy and this ring would have furnished us with all the necessaries of life so long as it was upon my finger. Alas! I have it no longer. What shall we do?"

"Dismiss all anxiety, dear mother," said Ourson. "Am I not tall and strong? I will seek for work and you can all live on my wages."

"And I, too," said Violette, "can I not assist my good

mother and Passerose? In seeking work for yourself, Ourson, you can also find something for me to do."

"I will go at once and seek work," said Ourson. "Adieu, mother. We will meet again, Violette."

Kissing their hands, he set off with a light step.

He had no presentiment, poor boy, of the reception which awaited him in the three houses where he sought employment.

THE FARM—THE CASTLE—THE FORGE

OURSON walked more than three hours before he arrived at a large and beautiful farm where he hoped to obtain employment. He saw from a distance the farmer and his family seated before his front door taking their evening meal.

He was but a short way off when one of the children, a little boy about ten years of age, perceived him. He sprang from his seat, uttered a cry of terror and fled into the house.

A second child, a little girl eight years old, hearing the cry of her brother turned towards Ourson and commenced the most piercing shrieks.

All the family now followed the movement of the children and turned around. At the sight of Ourson the women cried out with terror and the children fled in wild alarm. The men seized sticks and pitchforks expecting to be attacked by poor Ourson whom they took for some extraordinary animal escaped from a menagerie.

Ourson, seeing this movement of terror and preparation for attack, spoke to them hoping to dissipate their fears.

"I am not a bear, as you seem to suppose, but a poor boy seeking work and who would be very glad if you should give him employment."

The farmer was greatly amazed to hear a bear speak. He did not know whether to fly or to interrogate him further. He resolved, however, to speak.

"Who are you and from whence do you come?"

"I come from the Woodland Farm and I am the son of Agnella," Ourson replied.

"Ah, then it was you who in your childhood went with your mother to market and frightened all our children to death. You have lived in the woods and done without our help. Why do you seek us now? Go away and live as you have lived heretofore."

"Our farm-house is burned to the ground. I have to work now with my hands to support my mother and sister. For this reason, I pray you to give me work. I will do all you command me."

"Do you suppose, boy, that I will take into my service a villainous animal like you who will frighten my wife and my servants to death and throw my children into convulsions? I am not quite such a fool, my boy; not quite such a fool.

Enough of this. Be off, and allow us to finish our dinner."

"Master farmer, be merciful. Only try my work. Place me altogether by myself; then no one will fear me. I will conceal myself so well that your children shall not see me."

"Will you be done talking, wicked bear? Go instantly; if you don't you shall feel the teeth of my pitchfork."

Poor Ourson bowed his head. Tears of humiliation and disappointment glittered in his eyes. He withdrew slowly, followed by the coarse laugh and shouts of the farm hands.

When out of sight he no longer restrained his tears, but in all this shame and despair the thought that Violette could take upon herself his ugly covering did not enter his thoughts.

Ourson walked on till he came in sight of a castle where he saw a crowd of men coming, going and laboring at every kind of work. Some were mowing, some raking, some currying horses, some sweeping, some watering plants, some sowing.

"Here is a house where I shall certainly find work," said Ourson to himself. "I see neither women nor children and I think the men will not be afraid of me."

Ourson drew near without being seen. He took off his hat and stood before a man who seemed to be the superintendent.

"Sir—" said he.

The man looked up, recoiled a step when he saw Ourson and examined him with the greatest surprise.

"Who are you and what do you want?" said he, in a rude voice.

"Sir, I am the son of Agnella, mistress of the Woodland Farm."

"Well! and what has brought you here?"

"Our house is burned down, sir. I am seeking work in order to support my mother and sister. I hope you will be good enough to give me employment."

"Give employment to a bear?"

"Sir, I have only the appearance of a bear. Under this rough outside, which is so repugnant to you, there beats a human heart—a heart capable of gratitude and affection. You shall have no reason to complain either of my work or of my good will."

Whilst Ourson spoke and the superintendent listened with a mocking air, a great noise was heard amongst the horses. They began to kick and prance and the grooms could scarcely hold them. Some of them indeed escaped and fled in terror to the woods.

"It is the bear! It is the bear!" cried the grooms. "It has terrified the horses. Drive it off! Chase it away! We cannot control our horses."

"Off with you!" cried the superintendent.

Ourson was stupefied by his misfortunes and was immovable.

"Ha! you will not go," vociferated the man. "Wait a few moments, you hairy beast. I will give you something to run for. Halloa, men! bring out the dogs, and set them upon this animal. Hurry!—see him scampering off!"

In fact Ourson, more dead than alive at this cruel treatment, precipitately withdrew from the presence of these wicked and inhuman men. This second attempt had failed utterly but he would not allow himself to be discouraged.

"It is still three or four hours before sunset so I have time to continue my search for work."

He directed his steps towards a forge which was some distance from Woodland Farm. The master of the forge employed a great many workmen. He gave work to those who asked it, not in charity, but in view of his own interest. He was feared but he was not loved. He developed the riches of the country but no one thanked him for it because he alone profited by it. By his avidity and his opulence he ground down the poor workmen who could only find employment with this new Marquis of Carabas.

Poor Ourson arrrived at the forge. The master was at the door, scolding some, threatening others and terrifying all.

"Sir," said Ourson, drawing near, "have you any work to give me?"

"Certainly. What kind of work——?"

He raised his head at these words for he had replied without looking at Ourson. When his eye fell upon him he did not finish his phrase; his eyes flashed with rage and he stammered out:—

"What foolery is this? Are we in the midst of the Carnival, that a workman ventures upon such a ridiculous masquerade? Throw off your ugly bear's skin instantly or I will crisp your bristles for you in my fire."

"This, sir, is no masquerade," replied Ourson, sadly; "it is, alas! my natural skin but if you will be humane enough to employ me you will see that my strength is equal to my goodwill."

"I give work to you, you vile animal!" cried the master of the forge, foaming with rage: "I will put you into a sack and send you to a menagerie or I will throw you into a den with your brother bears. You will have work enough to defend yourself from their claws. Be off!"

And brandishing his club he would have dealt Ourson a heavy blow if the poor boy had not made a hasty retreat.

THE SACRIFICE

OURSON turned his steps homeward, discouraged and exhausted. He walked slowly and arrived at the farm late. Violette ran to meet him, took him by the hand, and without saying a word led him to his mother. There she fell on her knees and said:—

"My mother, I know what our well-beloved Ourson has suffered to-day. During his absence the fairy Furious has told me all and the good fairy Drolette has confirmed her story. My mother, when our Ourson was, as we believed, lost to us for ever and lost for my sake you revealed to me that which in his nobility and goodness he wished to conceal. I know that by changing skins with him I can restore to him his original beauty. Happy, a hundred times happy in having this opportunity to recompense the tenderness and devotion of my dearly-loved brother Ourson, I demand to make this exchange allowed by the fairy Drolette and I entreat her to complete the transfer immediately."

"Violette! Violette!" exclaimed Ourson, in great agitation, "take back your words! You do not know to what you engage yourself; you are ignorant of the life of anguish and misery unparalleled, the life of solitude and isolation to which you thus condemn yourself; you know not the unceasing desolation you will feel at knowing that you are an object of fear to all mankind. Violette, Violette, in pity to me, withdraw your words!"

"Dear Ourson," said Violette, calmly, but resolutely, "in making what you believe to be so great a sacrifice, I accomplish the dearest wish of my heart; I secure my own happiness; I satisfy an ardent and imperious desire to testify my tenderness and my gratitude. I esteem myself for doing what I propose. I should despise myself if I left it undone."

"Pause, Violette, for one instant longer, I beseech you! Think of my grief, when I no longer see my beautiful Violette, when I think of you exposed to the railleries, the horror of men. Oh! Violette, do not condemn your poor Ourson to this anguish."

The lovely face of Violette was veiled with sadness. The fear that Ourson would feel repugnance towards her made her heart tremble; but this thought, which was wholly personal, was very fleeting—it could not triumph over her devoted tenderness. Her only response was to throw herself in the arms of Agnella, and say:—

"Mother, embrace your fair and pretty Violette for the last time."

Whilst Agnella, Ourson and Passerose embraced her and looked lovingly upon her—whilst Ourson, on his knees, supplicated her to leave him his bear-skin to which he had been accustomed for twenty years—Violette called out again in a loud voice:—

"Fairy Drolette! Fairy Drolette! come and accept the price of the life and health of my dear Ourson."

At this moment the fairy Drolette appeared in all her glory. She was seated in a massive chariot of gold, drawn by a hundred and fifty larks. She was clothed with a robe of butterflies' wings, of the most brilliant colors while from her shoulders fell a mantle of network of diamonds, which trailed ten feet behind her and it was so fine in texture that it was light as gauze. Her hair, glittering like tissue of gold, was ornamented by a crown of carbuncles more brilliant than the sun; each of her slippers was carved from a single ruby and her beautiful face, soft, yet gay, breathed contentment. She fixed upon Violette a most affectionate regard.

"You wish it, then, my daughter?" said she.

"Madam," cried Ourson, falling at her feet, "deign to listen to me. You, who have loaded me with undeserved benefits—you, who have inspired me with boundless gratitude—you, good and just—will you execute the mad wish of my dear Violette? Will you make my whole life wretched by forcing me to accept this sacrifice? No, no, charming and humane fairy, you could not, you will not do it!"

Whilst Ourson was thus supplicating, the fairy gave Violette a light touch with her wand of pearl and Ourson another—then said:—

"Let it be according to the wish of your heart, my daughter. Let it be contrary to your ardent desires, my son."

At the same moment, the face, arms and the whole body of the lovely young girl were covered with the long hair which Ourson had worn, and Ourson appeared with a white smooth skin, which set off his extreme beauty to advantage.

Violette gazed at him with admiration, while he, his eyes cast down and full of tears, dared not look at his poor Violette, so horribly metamorphosed. At last he looked up, threw himself in her arms, and they wept together.

Ourson was marvellously handsome. Violette was, as Ourson had been, without form, without beauty, but not ugly. When Violette raised her head and looked at Agnella, the latter extended her hands towards her, and said:—

"Thanks, my daughter, my noble, generous child."

"Mother," said Violette, in low voice, "do you love me still?"

"Do I love you, my cherished child? Yes, a hundred times, a thousand times more than ever before."

"Violette," said Ourson, "never fear being ugly in our

eyes. To my eyes, you are a hundred times more beautiful than when clothed with all your loveliness. To me you are a sister—a friend incomparable. You will always be the companion of my life, the ideal of my heart."

THE COMBAT

VIOLETTE was about to reply, when a kind of roaring was heard in the air, and they saw descend a chariot made of crocodile's skin, drawn by fifty enormous toads. All the toads were hissing and blowing, and would have cast their infectious venom in every direction, if they had not been restrained by the power of the fairy Drolette.

When the chariot reached the ground, the fairy Furious, a huge and heavy creature, issued from it. Her big eyes seemed bursting from their sockets, her large flat nose covered her wrinkled, withered cheeks, her monstrous mouth extended from ear to ear and when it was open a long pointed black tongue was seen licking her horrid teeth.

She was not more than three feet in height and was very corpulent; her grizzly skin was gluey and cold, like a snail's and her thin red hair fell in locks of unequal length around her throat, which was disfigured by a goitre. Her large, flat hands looked like the fins of a shark, her dress was made of snail's skins and her mantle of the skins of toads.

She advanced towards Ourson (who shall hereafter be known by his true name of PRINCE MARVELLOUS) with a slow step. She paused in front of him and casting a furious glance upon the fairy Drolette and an eye of mocking triumph upon Violette, she folded her great cold arms and said in a sharp yet hoarse voice:—

"My sister has triumphed over me, Prince Marvellous. I have, however, one consolation: you will not be happy, because you have obtained your original beauty at the expense of that little fool, who is now frightful and repugnant and whom you will now never wish to approach. Yes! yes! weep, my handsome Ourson! You will weep a long time, Violette, and you will regret bitterly, if you do not already regret, that you have given your beautiful skin to the prince Marvellous."

"Never, madam, never! My only regret is that I did not know sooner what I could do to testify my gratitude."

The fairy Drolette, whose countenance had assumed an unaccustomed expression of severity and irritation, now waved her wand and said:—

"Silence, sister! You shall not triumph long over the misfortunes of Violette. I will provide a remedy for those misfortunes: her generous devotion merits recompense."

"I defy you to come to her assistance under penalty of my wrath," said Furious.

"I do not doubt your rage, sister, but I disdain to punish you for it," replied Drolette.

"To punish me!—Do you dare to threaten me?" said Furious. And hissing furiously, she called her chariot, mounted it, rose in the air and tried to launch upon Drolette all the venom of her toads in order to suffocate her.

But Drolette knew her sister perfectly. Her faithful larks held the door of her chariot open and she sprang within. The larks rose in the air, hovered above the toads, and then lowered themselves rapidly upon them. The toads, in spite of their weight, escaped the blows by turning adroitly to one side. They however threw their venom on the larks which were nearest to them, who died instantly.

Drolette detached them with the rapidity of a thunderbolt, rose again in the air and fell so adroitly on the toads, that the larks tore out their eyes with their claws, before Furious had time to come to the rescue of her army.

The outcries of the toads and the hissing of the larks made a deafening noise; and the fairy Drolette called out to her friends, who were regarding the combat with terror:—

"Withdraw immediately and stop your ears!"

Which was done instantly, in obedience to her command.

The fairy Furious made one last effort. She guided her

blinded toads in such a way as to meet the larks face to face, and to dart their venom upon them.

But Drolette rose higher and higher in the air and Furious found herself always under her sister's chariot.

At last, unable to contain her rage, Furious cried out:—

"You are assisted by the queen of the fairies, an old fool whom I should gladly see in the lower regions!"

Scarcely had she pronounced these words when her chariot fell heavily to the earth. The toads perished and the chariot disappeared. The fairy Furious only remained, in the form of an enormous toad. She wished to speak but she could only bellow and snuffle. She gazed at Drolette and her larks—at Prince Marvellous, Violette and Agnella, in a transport of rage but her power was destroyed.

The fairy Drolette lowered her chariot, descended to the earth and said:—

"The queen of the fairies has punished you for your audacity, sister. Repent, if you wish to obtain pardon."

The only answer of Furious was to spit forth her poisonous venom, which happily reached no one.

Drolette extended her wand towards her and said:

"I command you to disappear and never to appear again to the prince Marvellous, to Violette or to their mother."

Drolette had scarcely uttered these words when the toad disappeared; there remained no vestige of the chariot or of herself.

Drolette remained some time motionless. She passed her hand over her brow, as if to chase away a sad thought; then approaching Prince Marvellous, she said to him:—

"Prince, the title which I give you indicates your birth. You are the son of King Ferocious and the queen Aimee, concealed till now under the appearance of a modest farmer woman. The name of your father sufficiently indicates his character. Your mother having prevented him from killing his brother Indolent and his sister-in-law Nonchalante, he turned his rage against her. I was her protectress, and carried her off with her faithful Passerose in a cloud.

"And you, Princess Violette, your birth is equal to that of Prince Marvellous. Your father and mother were that same King Indolent and Queen Nonchalante who, saved once by Queen Aimee, became at last the victims of King Ferocious and their own apathy. Since that time King Ferocious has been killed by his subjects who could no longer support his cruel yoke.

"They expect you, prince, to reign over them. I have revealed to them your existence and I have promised them that you will take a wife worthy of you. You can select from the twelve princesses whom your father retained captive after having slain their parents. They are all wise and beautiful and each has a kingdom for her marriage portion."

Surprise had kept Prince Marvellous silent. At the

last words of the fairy he turned towards Violette, and seeing that she was weeping, he said:—

"Why do you weep, my Violette? Do you fear that I will blush for you—that I will not dare to testify before my whole court the tenderness with which you inspire me? That I will conceal what you have done for me or forget the bonds which attach me to you for ever? Can you believe that I will be ungrateful enough to seek any other affection than yours and fill your place by any of those princesses held captive by my father? No, dearest Violette! Until this time I have seen in you only a sister but from this moment you are the companion of my life, my sole friend, my wife!"

"Your wife, dear brother? That is impossible! How can you seat upon your throne a creature so repulsive as your poor Violette? How will you dare to brave the raillery of your subjects and of the neighboring kings? And how could I show my deformity in the midst of the festivals given on your return to your kingdom? No, no, my brother! Let me live near you, near to your mother, alone, unknown, covered with a veil. I cannot be your wife! No one shall blame you for having made so sad a choice."

The prince insisted long and firmly. Violette could scarcely control her emotions but she resisted with as much resolution as devotion. Agnella said nothing. She would have been willing that her son should accept even this last sacrifice from poor Violette and simply allow her to live near to them but hidden from the world.

Passerose wept and in a low tone encouraged the prince in his determination.

"Violette," said the prince, at last, "since you absolutely refuse to ascend the throne with me, I abandon it and all royal power in order to live with you as before in solitude and happiness. Without your sweet presence, the sceptre would be a heavy burden; with you at my side, our little farm will be a paradise! Say, dear Violette, shall it be so?"

"Yes, dear brother, you have triumphed; let us live as we have lived so many years: modest in our lives, happy in our affections."

"Noble prince and generous princess," said the fairy, "you shall be recompensed for this rare and devoted tenderness. Prince, in the well to which I carried you during the fire, there is a priceless treasure for Violette and yourself. Descend into the well, seek for it, and when you have found it bring it to me. I will teach you its value."

The prince did not wait to be told a second time; he ran towards the well; the ladder was still there and he descended. On arriving at the bottom, he saw nothing but the carpet which had been there from the first; he searched the walls of the well, but saw no indication of treasure. Finally he raised the carpet, and perceived a black stone with a ring attached; he raised the stone and discovered a casket which glittered like a constellation.

"This must contain the treasure spoken of by the fairy," said he.

The prince seized the casket; it was as light as a nutshell. He ascended the ladder hastily, holding the casket carefully in his arms.

They were awaiting his return with impatience. He handed the casket to the fairy. Agnella exclaimed:—

"This is the same casket you confided to me, madam, and which I supposed I had lost in the fire."

"It is the same," replied the fairy. "Here is the key; open it, prince."

Prince Marvellous hastened to open it. But who can describe the general disappointment, when, in place of some rich treasure which they supposed it contained, they found only the bracelets which Violette had worn when her cousin found her sleeping in the wood, and a vial of perfumed oil!

The fairy looked from one to the other, and enjoyed their surprise and consternation. She took the bracelets and gave them to Violette.

"This is my bridal present, my dear child; every one of these diamonds has the property of guarding from all evil influences the person who wears it, and of endowing its wearer with every virtue, enormous riches and resplendent beauty, with wit, intellect and all desirable happiness. Use them for the children who will be born of your union with Prince Marvellous.

"As to this vial of perfumed oil, it is the wedding gift of the prince your cousin. I know you love perfumes, this has peculiar virtues; use it to-day. To-morrow I will return to seek you and carry you all to your kingdom," she said.

"I renounce my kingdom, madam," said Ourson.

"Who will govern your people?" said Agnella.

"You, my mother, if you are willing," replied Ourson.

The queen was about to refuse, when the fairy interfered.

"We will speak of this to-morrow," said she. "You, madam, I know, desire to accept the crown which you are about to refuse. I forbid you, however, to accept it before my return. And you, dear and amiable prince," added she, in a sweet voice, accompanied with an affectionate glance, "I forbid you to repeat this offer before my return. Adieu till to-morrow. When you are truly happy, my dear children, think kindly of your friend the fairy Drolette."

The fairy ascended her chariot. The larks flew like lightning and she soon disappeared, leaving behind her a delicious perfume.

THE RECOMPENSE

PRINCE MARVELLOUS looked at Violette and sighed heavily; Violette gazed at the prince and smiled sweetly.

"How handsome you are, my dear cousin! I am so happy to have it in my power to restore you your beauty. And now I will pour some of this perfumed oil upon my hands; since I cannot please your eye, I will at least embalm you," said she, laughing.

She uncorked the vial, and entreated Marvellous to sprinkle some drops on her forehead and cheeks. The heart of the prince was too full for words. He took the vial and obeyed the order of his cousin. Their surprise and joy were indescribable on seeing that as soon as the oil touched Violette's forehead the hair disappeared and her skin resumed its original purity and dazzling whiteness.

The prince and Violette, on seeing the virtue of this

wonderful oil, uttered loud cries of delight and ran towards the stable where they saw Agnella and Passerose. They called their attention to the happy effect of this perfumed oil given them by the fairy. Both joined in their happiness. The prince could scarcely believe the evidence of his senses. And now nothing could prevent his union with Violette, so good, so devoted, so tender, so lovely, so well constituted to make him supremely happy.

The queen thought of the morrow—of her return to her kingdom, which she had abandoned twenty years ago. She wished that she herself, that Violette, that her son the prince had clothing worthy of so great an occasion but, alas! she had neither the time nor the means to procure them: they would therefore be compelled to wear their coarse clothing, and thus show themselves to their people. Violette and Marvellous laughed at this distress of their mother.

"Do you not think, mamma," said Violette, "that our dear prince is sufficiently adorned with his rare beauty and that a rich and royal robe would not make him more beautiful or more amiable?"

"And do you not agree with me, my dear mother," said Marvellous, "in thinking that our dear Violette is lovely enough in the simplest clothing, that the lustre of her eyes surpasses the most brilliant diamonds, that the clear whiteness of her teeth rivals successfully the rarest pearls, that the richness of her blonde hair surpasses a crown of brilliants?"

"Yes, yes, my children," replied Agnella, "without doubt, you are both of you handsome and attractive but a rich dress spoils nothing, not even beauty. Jewels, embroidery and heavy brocades would detract nothing from your charms. And I who am old——"

"But not ugly, madam," interrupted Passerose, hastily. "You are still amiable and handsome, in spite of your little country cap, your skirts of coarse striped cloth, your waist of red camlet and your stomacher of simple cloth. Besides, when you return to your kingdom, you can buy every kind of dress your heart desires."

The evening passed away gayly and there seemed no anxiety about the future. The fairy had provided their supper; they passed the night on the bundles of hay in the stable and as they were all fatigued by the emotions of the day they slept profoundly. The sun had been shining a long time and the fairy Drolette was with them, before they awoke.

A soft "Hem! hem!" of the fairy aroused them. The prince was the first to open his eyes; he threw himself on his knees before the fairy and thanked her with such warmth and gratitude that her heart was touched.

Violette was on her knees by his side and joining her thanks to those of the prince.

"I do not doubt your gratitude, dear children," said the fairy; "but I have much to do. I am expected in the kingdom of the king Benin where I am to attend at the birth of the third son of the princess Blondine. This prince is to be the husband of your first daughter, Prince Marvellous, and I am resolved to endow him with all the qualities which will obtain for him the warm love of your daughter. And now I must conduct you to your kingdom; I will return in time to be present at your wedding. Queen," she continued, turning to Aimee, who was now just opening her eyes, "we are about to set out immediately for your son's kingdom. Are you and your faithful Passerose ready for the journey?"

"Madam," replied the queen, with a slight embarrassment, "we are ready to follow you but will you not blush for our dress, so little worthy of our rank?"

"It is not I who will blush, queen," said the fairy, smiling, "but rather yourself who have this sensation of shame. But I will remedy this evil also."

Saying this, she described a circle with her wand above the head of the queen, who in the same moment found herself clothed in a robe of gold brocade. Upon her head was a hat with splendid plumes, fastened with a band of superb diamonds and her boots were of velvet, spangled with gold.

Aimee looked at her robe with an air of complaisance.

"And Violette and my son the prince, will you not extend your goodness to them also?"

"Violette and the prince have asked for nothing. I will do as they wish. Speak, Violette, do you desire to change your costume?"

"Madam," replied Violette, casting down her sweet eyes and blushing, "I have been sufficiently happy in this robe of simple cloth. In this costume my brother knew me and loved me. Permit me to continue to wear it as far as regard for my station allows and allow me to preserve it always in remembrance of the happy years of my childhood."

The prince thanked Violette for these sweet words, and pressed her hand tenderly.

The fairy kindly nodded her approval and called for her chariot, which was waiting a few steps from them. She entered and placed the queen next herself, then the prince, Violette and Passerose.

In less than an hour the larks had flown over the three thousand leagues which separated them from the kingdom of Prince Marvellous. All his court and all his subjects, apprised beforehand by the fairy, expected him. The streets and the palaces were filled by the eager, happy crowd.

When the chariot appeared in sight, the people uttered cries of joy which were redoubled when it drew up before the great entrance of the palace, when they saw descend Queen Aimee, a little older, no doubt, but still pretty and gracious, and the Prince Marvellous, whose natural beauty and grace were enhanced by the splendor of his clothing, glittering with gold and precious stones, which were also a present from the fairy.

But the acclamations arose to frenzy when the prince,

taking Violette by the hand, presented her to the people.

Her sweet, attractive countenance, her superb and elegant form, were adorned with a dress with which the fairy had clothed her by one stroke of her wand.

Her robe was of gold lace, while her waist, her arms and shoulders shone with innumerable larks formed of diamonds larger than humming-birds. On her graceful head she wore a crown of larks made of precious stones of all colors. Her countenance, soft but gay, her grace, her beauty, won the hearts of all.

For a long time nothing was heard but shouts of "Long live King Marvellous! Long live Queen Violette!" The noise and tumult were so great that many persons became deaf. The good fairy, who desired that only joy and happiness should prevail throughout the kingdom on this auspicious day, cured them instantly at the request of Violette.

There was a magnificent feast spread for the court and the people. A million, three hundred and forty-six thousand, eight hundred and twenty-two persons dined at the expense of the fairy and each guest was permitted to carry away enough for eight days.

During the repast the fairy set off for the kingdom of King Benin, promising to return in time for the wedding of Marvellous and Violette. During the eight days of the fairy's absence Marvellous, who saw that his mother was a little sad at not being queen, entreated her earnestly to accept

Violette's kingdom and she consented to reign there on condition that King Marvellous and Queen Violette would come every year and pass three months with her.

Queen Aimee, before parting with her children, wished to witness their marriage. The fairy Drolette and many other fairies of her acquaintance and many genii were invited to the marriage. They all received the most magnificent presents, and were so satisfied with the welcome given them by King Marvellous and Queen Violette that they graciously promised to return whenever they were invited.

Two years afterwards they received an invitation to be present at the birth of the first child of King Marvellous. There came to Queen Violette a daughter, who, like her mother, was a marvel of goodness and beauty.

The king and queen could not fulfil the promise they had made to Queen Aimee. One of the genii who had been invited to the wedding of Marvellous and Violette, found in Queen Aimee so much of goodness, sweetness, and beauty, that he loved her, and, visiting her several times in her new kingdom and being affectionately and graciously received by her, he carried her off one day in a whirlwind. Queen Aimee wept for a while but as she loved the genius she was not inconsolable; indeed, she promptly consented to wed him. The king of the genii granted to her as a wedding present the power of participating in all the privileges of her husband: never to die, never to grow old and the ability to transport herself in the twinkling of an eye wherever she wished to go. Aimee used this power very often to visit her son and his children.

King Marvellous and Queen Violette had eight sons and four daughters and they were all charming. They were happy, without doubt, for they loved each other tenderly and their grandmother, who, it was said spoiled them a little induced their grandfather, the genius Bienveillant, to contribute all in his power to their happiness. Consequently, they received many rich gifts.

Passerose, who was warmly attached to Queen Aimee, had followed her into her new kingdom but when the genius carried her off in a whirlwind, Passerose, seeing herself forgotten and not being able to follow her mistress was so sad in the loneliness caused by the departure of Aimee, that she prayed the fairy Drolette to transport her to the kingdom of King Marvellous and Queen Violette. She remained with them and took care of their children to whom she often recounted the adventures of Ourson and Violette. She still remains, it is said, though the genius and his queen have made her many excuses for not having carried her off in the whirlwind.

"No, no," Passerose replied to all these explanations; "let us remain as we are. You forgot me once—you might forget me another time. Here, my dear Ourson and my sweet Violette never forget their old nurse. I love them and

I will remain with them. They loved me and they will take care of me."

The farmer, the superintendent, and the master of the forge who had been so cruel to Ourson were severely punished by the fairy Drolette.

The farmer was devoured by a bear, some hours after he had chased away Ourson.

The superintendent was dismissed by his master for having let loose the dogs, who escaped and never could be found. The same night he was bitten by a venomous serpent and expired some moments afterwards.

The master of the forge having reprimanded his workmen too brutally, they resolved upon vengeance: seized him and cast him into the blazing furnace where he perished miserably.

Printed in the United States
30179LVS00005B/86

9 781410 105691